The Power & The Glory

A Vatican subversion

by

C.H.Elton

About the author

C.H.Elton is the penname of a part-time author who is married, and lives in the North-West of England where they have 5 children and 3 grandchildren (at the moment). A prolific writer of poetry and various forms of fiction since schooldays, Through Fear and Love is the first of his crime thriller novels to be published.

This debut novel is a crime thriller based around the fictional characters from Neerdorf Securities (NL) and their imagined interaction with the Catholic Church and a corrupt senior Cardinal. Hopefully you will enjoy the journey and if so, it would be greatly appreciated if you would consider leaving a small review on Amazon.

See more on his Amazon author page at http:/author.amazon.co.uk or come and say hello on Twitter – sdc130764 (C H Elton author)

You can contact the author by email c/o – SDCPrestonPress@aol.com

C.H.Elton has also independently self-published, via Amazon Kindle Direct Publishing, a collection of 6 short story monologues titled, 'Reflections – monologues and muses of modern times'. It tells the tales of six unrelated characters who speak from the heart about their situations and how they got to be where they are.

Chapter 1

Nena drifted out over the peaceful stillness that existed around the pool and over the nearby beach. Apparently, 99 red balloons go by. None of the sun-soaked bodies seemed to care as they lie under canopies searching for shade and a modicum of protection from the unrelenting power of the sun. Others of course relished the burning sensation it created. Some craved it and followed it around its daytime arc hanging onto its every ray under the illusion of protection from bottles of SPF 8. No-one however appeared to have any concerns or had an awareness about anything around their own two-square metres of sun-lounger holiday space other than an occasional paperback and a white wine spritzer. George Michael now reckons that 'all he wants right now is you!' Funny that isn't. He had all of those swooning girls back in the 80's hanging on his every word and deed, and as it turned out probably being a little bit devastated in the 90's when it became clearer who the 'you' was.

Anita and Gert blended into the relaxed holiday scene perfectly well, that is of course why they had been chosen. Both in their mid-50's and a little too sunburned suggesting they had so far enjoyed a more than comfortable lifestyle. To anyone remotely interested, they appeared for all the world as a well matured couple (matured in the sense of good wine), existing in the perfect union they had created and had vowed to nurture over 20 years earlier in a small church on the outskirts of Düsseldorf. Well-travelled sun seekers, enjoying the companionship that a long-term love affair ultimately results in. They carried it off absolutely, as it was true, and having completed three other missions in the last year, they were confident, comfortable and looking forward to a year off once this assignment was completed.

Dirk Neerdorf is a successful Dutch investment banker responsible for the lending facility and the ultimate controlling shareholder of Neerdorf Securities (Netherlands) Limited. NSL is a relatively secretive organisation in terms of its structure and its lending policies, working by a philosophy of zero marketing spend, all its business being generated by word of mouth on a strictly need to know basis. Its clientele was generally, below the radar multinationals, if such a thing exists and high net worth individuals who might need to get their hands on some cash and would prefer a degree of anonymity, especially where their financial affairs are concerned. NSL supported big companies with big budget needs, who like itself, would rather be out of the limelight and definitely out of the media. Right now, Dirk was on the dreamy Greek Island of Kos and, through no fault of his own, his world and that of his bank, was all about to change.

Over the past two days Anita and Gert had acted out their vacation whilst observing very closely the movements of Neerdorf, hoping to identify some habits or at least routine movements. Experience told them that almost everyone created, often subconscious routines when away from home, especially when that was on a luxury holiday complex with all the distractions to experience. The trio had already interacted on a few occasions, exchanging pleasantries, smiles, nods of recognition. The sort of things that happen in the early stages of any holiday as like minds seek each other out for comfort and entertainment purposes later in the break. For the couple, this was the easiest of tasks as being a man of meticulous perfection, Neerdorf ran his life with the steady rhythm of a Swiss watch. At exactly 6ft tall, weighing it at exactly 175 lbs, his perfect olive tan carried before him an image of knowledge, power and sophistication that was the envy of anyone who he came into contact with. His absolute charmer of a smile and slight but refined muscle tones brought longing gazes from both sexes and in someone else could have easily led to a debauched lifestyle to rival any. Neerdorf however, was a man of principle and honour. God fearing in its traditional sense he was dedicated to his Christian beliefs and true to his loving wife of 30 years and their 25-year-old twin sons. He knew that nothing would ever lead him astray from his single minded, righteous path, even if his business dealings did bring him close to areas of the world and into direct contact with characters he would otherwise avoid. He often reminded himself and his sons, who were co-directors and shareholders in the business, that it suited them to know the workings of the devil so as to know how to avoid its temptation. After all, whilst God had created man in his own image, He has also allowed His people a freedom to develop, explore and express itself in many different ways and as such, that was the way of the world.

Two days earlier, Dirk had left Rome's Leonardo Da Vinci airport for Athens. Historically, two hugely important cities throughout the development of the modern world and in part, responsible for its cultural evolution. Both cities accountable for innovation, progress and conflict in equal measure over the centuries. A fact not lost on a troubled Neerdorf as he sat contemplating a very difficult and morally troubling meeting, he'd attended earlier that day in the heart of one of the world's most historic cities. Five years earlier, at the same venue, he had readily agreed to sign off the biggest finance deal his firm had ever seen; a draw down facility of $100m supported by arguably the safest securities that existed anywhere in the world.

The money of course was not all his, it had been generated and guaranteed using a combination of large European banks and other financial institutions with varying degrees of cost and risk. In truth though, there was no risk as providing this level of finance, making available ready cash to the Vatican was probably the safest loan he'd ever made. The Catholic church, with all its collateral value, moral fortitude and worldwide support meant it was considered a low-grade risk and very easy to secure support for; it was as close to a sure-fire winner as you could get.

'But why do they need so much Father, and why from us?' Neerdorf remembered the question posed by his eldest son of 15 minutes at the approvals committee.
'Erik,' Neerdorf had responded quietly and confidently, 'the church sees us as morally compatible with their aims and beliefs. In this transaction we have been asked by God himself to help launch the next phase in the growth of Christianity across the world.' A smile of immense pride etched across his features 'we shouldn't question the wishes of God Erik; we simply ensure that our governance rules are met and then help where we can'
'what's your view Thomas?' Erik turned to face his brother
'I think father is right, we manage our risk and answer to our shareholders, it shouldn't matter whether this is the Catholic church or the Playboy mansion, if they satisfy the criteria, our guiding principle is to lend and secure. It is without question a large transaction, but their rationale and demonstration of need is perfectly acceptable. Plus, the return for our shareholders is very attractive and we have a duty to do what's best for them.'
Dirk smiled, his youngest son was by far the most pragmatic of the two other members of the committee and he had been proved right time and again to have made him Chief Operating Officer. It wasn't a difficult choice in truth, the hard bit was the conversation with Erik. The role of Relationship Director and a 200,000 Euro salary made it easier however and made best use of Erik's extrovert nature and brilliant social awareness. If anyone was born to exist into a world of corporate hospitality, Erik was that person.
'ok, for the record, are we unanimous?' Dirk studied his two co-directors, they both nodded ascent and the meeting was closed.

'I still feel a bit awkward though' Erik stood and left the room.
'No need to minute that last bit Thomas' Dirk smiled
'The minutes are already closed dad'.

As he sat 35,000 feet up in the air entering Greek airspace the cautious note of his eldest son re-entered his memory like a ghostly apparition. The fact was, over the past year almost all of the draw down facility had been called upon and there had been late repayments in four of the last six months. Even more concerning, last month's repayment was still in default. Dirk had no other option and therefore decided to visit the Vatican again for three reasons; 1) collect the default in cash, 2) remind the Holy See of its repayment obligations and 3) review its securities. Part one had gone unexpectedly well, he had in his case $5m cash, handed to him even before he had taken his seat at the table with the two Cardinals. Alberto Brazi was Chief Finance Officer in the Holy city, reporting directly to the Pope himself. He was a meek, softly spoken gentle man, his close-fitting robes and overall demeanour fitted a man of the cloth well. He is a man you could talk with and trust, his heart was filled with God and his every action promoted the Christian values he feared, adored and lived by. Sat next to him, and by complete contrast, was the huge menacing figure of Georges De Cathay, the highest-ranking Frenchman in Vatican City and Head of Legal Office. His size didn't betray his nature either as he was in reality a brutish bully feared by most people who knew and dealt with him. His reputation was filled with stories of fierce violent outbursts, kidnappings, disappearances and even a rumour of murder. Dirk was uncomfortable in this environment, with this unnatural giant of a man, and it was one of the few occasions that led him to question his faith; how a man of God, and a very senior one at that, could have such a reputation. If they were true, how could he possibly serve the values and traditions of the church, the very things that he preached daily and had taken an oath to.

The cash exchange had been easy, it took Cardinal Brazi less that ten minutes to count the cash, feeding it into the automated note counter and loading it into the case, handing the confirmation note to Dirk. There had been no apology or explanation, it was simply a straightforward cash transaction. A large one for sure and one which made Dirk unusually nervous, but it happened and passed without contention or debate. Dirk closed the case, placed it by his side and took a seat.
'There is something else Mr Neerdorf?' Brazi smiled in that saintly way only a man of the cloth can and bowed his head slightly in pseudo subservience. There was no doubt who held the power in this room though. Dirk looked across the heavy oak table towards the two priests 'my agenda, as you both know, is three-fold Cardinal Brazi'
'We had rather hoped that our demonstration of support for our continued relationship would satisfy all of your requests' De Cathay interjected; his deep voice resonated with absolute authority.
Dirk thought for a few seconds, considering the implications of that response. He decided to continue after all, he wasn't being unreasonable, especially given the circumstances and the amounts involved. 'Gentlemen, please don't be offended, I simply have protocols to follow, rules to satisfy, shareholders to answer to, surely you can appreciate that?'
'Mr Neerdorf...' De Cathay had clearly taken over proceedings now that the cash had been handed over, 'you will agree, no doubt, that we have just demonstrated to you and the majority shareholding of NSL that we are secure and able to meet our obligations. You have just taken receipt of $2.5m representing the correction of an accounting error along with $2.5m to meet this current month's obligation in advance' the words were emphasised 'and this clearly demonstrates that we have available funds and are secure Mr Neerdorf. The trust we show in your organisation should not be underestimated.' Both holy men smiled in

unison, expecting the conversation and the meeting to be over. Dirk however knew he just couldn't leave without the complete fulfilment of part two and three of his request.

'I am very clear and very flattered to receive your trust; however, I have a duty to ensure my firms investments are secure. I don't think my request is unreasonable and I have given sufficient notice of these requirements so as to expect them to be met or at the very least, be given advance notice that I.....' he stopped to choose his words carefully, knowing that at least one of the men he was addressing was capable of irrational, hot headed reactions. He decided on 'may have to wait a short while.' Dirk remained seated and on the outside at least, appeared cool and calm. His heart however was thundering deep inside his chest and his palms were not just moist, they were wet! Georges took a seat at the head of the table 'Dirk...' he used his first name, his Christian name for the opening round of this phase of the meeting 'what you ask, causes us a problem. You can't surely be doubting us, we have shown you we are strong. We give you assurances and our personal guarantees. Need I remind you of our authority here Dirk? We trust you and recognise your faith, we have always been good business partners and have enjoyed an honest, open relationship this last five years. Dirk, you should accept the word of the Christian church today as you did all those years ago. Nothing has changed and I can offer you my personal guarantee on behalf of His Holiness and God himself.' An anxious looking Brazi had moved to stand behind his colleague and business partner. Dirk sensed immediately that there was a problem, he had over 30 years' experience in this business and recognised desperation and deceit very easily and here it appeared to him as clear as the sky, in the very place it was supposed to be most alien. Dirk was worried. His heart told him that he was dealing with God, what right did he have to question the thing he revered the most, but his head was screaming, red alert!! Had this meeting been with any other of his customers he'd now give seven days' notice to provide sight of the securities he sought or face foreclosure.

'Cardinal' he decided to remain formal 'you will recognise that, like you, my position comes with responsibility. I wouldn't dare suggest that mine comes close to the magnitude that your position carries, but nonetheless, I have to answer to my conscience, my shareholders, and my other customers. My trinity if you like' Dirk smiled at his own attempt to inject a little light humour ' I need to satisfy myself that they are protected and that our investment is secure, the only way I can do that is to see first-hand that the collateral worth attached to that investment is sufficient should it ...er...fail...' the enormity of the sentence hit all three attendees at the same time

De Cathay rose sharply sending Brazi backwards, his face had become red with the rage for which he was famous. His huge hand curled into a sledge like fist and slammed down into the ancient dark wood of the table 'Fail!?!' his voice carried over the large expanse of the room and out into the corridors that enveloped this room that had dated back to at least 1100 A.D. 'you fucking imbecile, how the hell do you imagine that the most powerful organisation on Earth can fail' his eyes bulged and seemed to roll upwards back into his round block of a head 'this place you sit in and mock Mr Neerdorf is the centre of the Roman Catholic empire, it is omnipotent, majestic and fucking secure. It answers only to God my friend, you remember that, it answers ONLY TO GOD HIMSELF!' the words echoed around the expanse of the chamber. De Cathay stood there shaking with rage and disbelief at what he was witnessing, Neerdorf remained sat, calm, showing no signs of the turmoil that was ripping through his head and the blood coursing through his veins at an alarming rate, pumping his heart faster than is good for anyone. Brazi spoke first, quietly, and hesitantly 'perhaps we should take a break, would you like a coffee Mr Neerdorf?'

'perhaps we should finish' interjected De Cathay in a rasping, forced whisper 'we are done are we not Mr Neerdorf?' Dirk gripped the arms of his chair showing for the first time, tense signs of anxiety 'no, I think we should continue' he spoke to the centre of the table, averting the gaze of the two men who stood staring at him in disbelief 'I need sight of the agreed covenants within seven days. For absolute clarity that means, proof of ownership of each and every building that was put up as collateral against your facility. According to my records, that relates to three buildings in Vatican City, two more outside the walls in Rome and one property in Paris, France.'

The two men regarded Dirk, open mouthed, one ashen faced and wide eyed, the other bright purple with blood red eyes which in that moment depicted nothing but pure evil. ' you will consider foreclosing on the church? Do you appreciate what it is you are involved in here! I think, Mr Neerdorf, you will pick up your case and return to your family in that nice home on the outskirts of Amsterdam. You will do this, and you will tell everyone that your business with Rome is satisfactory Mr Neerdorf' the words spat and hissed out of De Cathay with a menace Dirk had never encountered before. 'I will bid you farewell; I doubt we will meet again' De Cathay offered his hand. Dirk remained seated hands flat on the cold surface of the wooden table in front of him 'I'm sorry gentlemen, I seem not to have made my request clear' he reached down to his document case and placed it in front of him. Trying desperately to steady his hands he opened it and extracted a printed document, handing it to Brazi. The priest looked at it quizzically and before he had chance to ask, Dirk explained 'it's a formal request for the documents I just asked for, it gives you seven days from today to provide the original documents. I'm going to Greece for a few days, can I suggest a conference call in three days by way of an update?' Dirk passed over a hotel card 'you can get me on the number I've written on the back'

De Cathay moved towards the door 'you're a fool Mr Neerdorf, you can't possibly imagine the dangers that exist in this dark world' he left Dirk alone with Alberto Brazi and an uneasy silence. 'Forgive my colleague Mr Neerdorf, he is very........passionate, in his protection of our church'

Dirk stood, collected his cases and made his way in silence with Brazi out of the room and through a series of corridors to an unmarked exit.

'take care Mr Neerdorf'

'I'll await your call Mr Brazi'

Dirk found himself in a courtyard looking at a heavy iron gateway onto a busy main road. He stood for a moment, steadying himself, catching his breath, quickly going over the past hour in his swirling head, the concerns and the threats. He spent the next few minutes clearing the sick from his mouth as he vomited into the row of bushes lining the way to the gateway, careful not to mark his shoes or suit, he then walked out onto the street, hailed a cab and headed towards the airport.

Chapter 2

The Head of Security at the Vatican is 45-year-old Paul Hindle, Paolo to his friends of which there were many. He was by nature a very amiable character who saw good in everyone. An irony not lost on his colleagues but an irony that he often demonstrated was flawed. His parents were English and very successful, managing to make their huge fortune upon the sale of the family steel works business in their hometown near Sheffield in the late 70's. They moved to Italy before Paul was born, settling on the outskirts of Rome in a gated mansion residence that stood out even in a neighbourhood occupied by Oligarch's, film starts and minor royalty. His upbringing was a paradoxical mix of frugality borne of his Yorkshire heritage and the flamboyance and luxury of the Italian high life. In his early teens Paul quickly realised that the opulent extravagance he had taken for granted was not his by right and after some soul searching and disagreement with his parents, had decided to follow his calling into the church. He entered college at 16 and was ordained at 26 making him one of the youngest practicing priests in the church. Thereafter his success came very quick, some would say influenced by his friendship with another fast-rising star, Georges De Cathay. When challenged by this Paul was always quick to add that he wouldn't be in his position unless he could demonstrate his competence, and everyone had to accept that without question. His forthright approach and Italian styling produced in him an engaging, charming personality along with an incredible almost spiritual intuition. His special skill was in the way he questioned or interrogated people with a warm smile that created a sense of casual, relaxed conversation and this allowed him to manipulate peers and subordinates alike. It was this ability that made him highly competent and valued but it also allowed him to move up the ranks as he uncovered and recorded many indiscretions amongst the halls and chambers of the walled City.

It wasn't entirely unusual for Paul to be summoned to see De Cathay this early in the week, it was normally a pleasure left for Thursdays or Friday morning when they had their routine catch-up. Tuesday was normally the day Paul checked out which girls were available to be working in the city and would be around and willing to pander to De Cathay's whims each Saturday. De Cathay had a penchant for young looking girls and paid handsomely for a few hours of their company, entertaining them in a secret chamber deep beneath street level, far away from tourists and other prying eyes. This Tuesday however, Paul was actually going to see his friend Georges. Paul entered the 13th century building and made his way through the wooden clad corridor, passing rooms he rarely had cause to enter but always admiring the ancient architecture that was ever present in these chambers. Behind these doors were the workplaces of some of the most powerful men in the Christian church, Holy men of God charged with running and expanding the faith across the whole world. At the head of the long row of identical doors, immediately before the huge double entrance to the chapel was an imposing solid oak door which carried the mark 'GDC – Head of Legal Affairs'. Paul knocked lightly and entered, not waiting to be invited in. He was probably the only person, including His Holiness, who dared but he had known Georges for a very long time. De Cathay was stood with his back to the door looking out of the large picture window that afforded a magnificent view of the gardens. He was whispering instructions into the phone and continued with his conversation as he turned and beckoned Paul to take a seat. As he waited, Paul sensed a tension in the air and noted the fire in his colleagues' eyes. It didn't faze him however as he had of course seen it many times over the years. He knew he was going to be given a job to do, all Paul wondered was when, how and who. The phone went down gently, and De Cathay looked across at his protege 'Paolo, my friend, how are you and how is the Holy Secret Service' it was a predictable greeting and one which Georges found amusing. To the outside world, Vatican Security amounted to a small, select group of policemen in ceremonial costume, performing ritualistic duties for the benefit of tourists. In practice, and to those who lived and worked inside the sacred walls, it was a highly organised, secretive service that stretched across the globe. Paul controlled it all from his seat in Rome and enjoyed every minute.

'I'm very well Georges thank you and so are my people. What about you? I'm not accustomed to visiting so early in the day or the week come to that, do we have a problem?' De Cathay smiled, he preferred this style of approach, it made much more sense and was easier to understand than the language of religious diplomacy that was the norm in these buildings. Georges felt that some Vatican employees, especially the older and more senior, thought it necessary to speak in what he referred to as riddles, masking opinion and even general conversation in double meaning and old age bibliographical terminology. 'you are so direct Paolo, so refreshing and of course so intuitive. There is a small matter I need your help with'

Paul studied his friend and could see that this 'small matter' was clearly more important than Georges wished to admit at this time. When agitated, De Cathay's give away sign was the slight involuntary tick to his lower eye lid 'happy to help as always' Paul offered ' what can I do for you?'

'I need to confirm some details Paolo, we have business with a Dutch financier, and it has become necessary to update our information relating to him for security reasons.'

Paul of course knew of the arrangement with NSL, it was part of his role five years earlier to investigate the firm and gather as much intelligence as possible. It was noted at that time by the investigation team that the three directors were related, the owner was squeaky clean as was the younger twin Thomas. The elder one, Erik, had some interesting history that might be useful if needed to influence decisions later in the business relationship. He also knew that 'security reasons' had many meanings. Only a few months earlier it had meant gathering 'evidence' against a prominent British bookmaker, ahead of reaching an amicable arrangement to clear a substantial gambling debt built up by one of the senior clergymen in Ireland. 'Yes, ok Georges, I think I recall who you mean. What am I looking for?'

'We had a residential address for the majority shareholder, I need someone to visit and confirm that it is still correct, and that this man's family still reside there with him – that is his wife and two sons. Paolo this has to be done quietly, no noise, no trace'

'Of course, Georges, it will be completed before the week is out...' a sharp rap on the door broke into the conversation 'come' ordered Georges in that deep authoritative voice. A familiar face to both appeared 'Alberto, how nice to see you, come in take a seat'

Paul made to stand up 'No stay. We haven't yet finished; Alberto and I have no secrets to keep from our Head of Security' he turned and glanced with a smile towards the slight frame of the man entering the room. 'Come both of you, sit' he offered his hand across the solid desk topped with a deep, aged red leather. The desk was tidy, empty, apart from the phone and ornamental Mont Blanc silver pen in a gold edged marble holder. Brazi hesitated slightly and then acknowledged Paul with a courteous nod and handshake

'It is about yesterday's meeting Georges; I need to speak with you'

Georges considered his counterpart with a steely gaze 'Good, you've arrived at the right time. It's all being sorted out Alberto, our friend Paolo is undertaking some research for us although, I haven't yet spoken with him about getting the money back but we can do that now if you like' De Cathay continued to eye Alberto with a domineering stare

'What money?' Paul's features tensed, Brazi turned to look Paul square in the face. Paul thought his colleague looked nervous, ashen almost 'Alberto, are you ok?'

'We have a.....erm...situation. We need you to do some work for us' Brazi was almost whispering 'something has come up that needs urgent attention. To satisfy the needs of the

Dutch financier and his company, the church has had to....' he thought carefully then continued 'provide documentary evidence that there is sufficient value available within the church to meet our financing obligations'

Paul looked blankly, thinking carefully 'and what does that mean exactly' realising that his earlier observation of Georges had indeed been accurate

'It means' Brazi continued 'we have had to give them...'

'for the love of God, Alberto, stop dithering just spit it out! Paolo, we have to provide proof of our collateral guarantees and we have had to give NLS a substantial cash deposit, we need that back before the weekend'

Paul knew not to ask how much but just couldn't help himself 'and what is 'substantial'?'

Georges laughed at the direct question from his friend 'more than we can afford to let go at this moment in time and more than is healthy for some people'

Brazi handed Paul a hotel card 'this is where you will find the money tomorrow morning, the Dutchman will be there for a few days we understand'

Paul took it and noted the phone number on the back 'looks like I'll be busy then' he smiled

'Yes indeed' De Cathay responded, 'there is another requirement Paolo, we need to be very certain that our Dutch friend will not be returning to our city'. The meaning was immediately clear. Paul considered the conversation without emotion; this wasn't the first time Georges had made such a request and he already knew a good 'disposal' expert. 'ok, I'll keep you informed of progress when I can' Paul rose from the heavily carved chair, nodded at both men and left for his own office. As he walked over the half mile of crossed corridors, Paul was happy with his decision to work away from this part of the building. Sometimes he didn't like the atmosphere around the other head of department offices.

Back in De Cathay's office the other two men waited a few minutes to make sure they remained alone. 'is it really necessary Georges, surely we don't need to have him killed' Brazi clutched at his rosary beads as he spoke, his eyes avoiding the gaze of his fellow holy man

'You know it as well as I do Alberto, God's will isn't always as black and white as we would all like it to be. Our duty is to protect the workings of our church and sometimes this involves doing things that some other people would struggle to understand.' he paused and took a deep breath, 'in our service to God, we both know what needs to be done and we also know we do it with the Lords blessing' Georges spoke solemnly and with authority, Alberto bowed his head got up from his seat and moved towards the door. 'Alberto, our faith is our life and with both we serve our God, be under no illusion that what needs to done will be done and that you will be with me as we resolve this issue' without responding or looking up, Brazi moved through the doorway and quickly shuffled down the corridor and into the gardens. After a minute he stopped and fell to his knees, lifting his bronze crucifix to his lips he whispered 'holy father, I beg for your guidance and forgiveness, please help me to survive this awful situation that has been created'. For the second time that day, someone vomited in the Vatican courtyard.

Georges remained in his office and observed Alberto's departure from the building on his CCTV monitor. 'Alberto, you are so weak, what am I going to do with you?' He made a mental note to speak with Paulo.

Dirk had landed in Athens after a very smooth flight and had passed through customs unchallenged with both of his carry-on cases. Money definitely talked in some areas of life, and it had indeed smoothed his exit on this occasion. It was surprising what 200 euro could achieve when handed to the right official. A short taxi ride followed by a very pleasant hour on a ferry to the isle of Kos had changed Neerdorf's state of mind considerably. He was starting to relax. Arriving at his luxury apartment overlooking the sea, he poured himself a glass of champagne from the half bottle he had ordered on his way to the holiday village. Placing the bottle back in the ice bucket he picked up his phone and pressed speed-dial no.1, Thomas answered.

'Hi dad, how's Kos?' his son's naturally calming voice was always a tonic to Dirk

'Hi son, good thanks, as always great to hear you'

'good, good, and how was the meeting?'

'it was fine' he lied 'part one completed, and I'll finish the other parts in a few days'

'really? Was there a problem?'

'no just a misunderstanding, I'm going to view the documents before the weekend. Nothing for us to worry about though. How's mum?'

'Mum is good too, looking forward to coming out to see you next week. We're all having dinner together tomorrow, Erik has invited one of the firm's lawyers over as a sweetener to a deal he's doing, I think he's expecting a big bill coming from them so he's showing them that we can't afford to eat out'. Both men laughed.

'Thomas, I'll call you tomorrow, same time. I just have to make another call, then I'm off to bed for an hour, it's been a long day'

'sure dad, no worries take care'. The phones went dead. Thomas sat for a moment concerned that his father had just lied to him and worried about what was going wrong with the Catholic Church Account.

Dirk made his next call immediately 'I need an armed secure collection to arrange a significant deposit into our account please' he listened to the instructions he was given before confirming his address and identification code. 'ok. one hour, I'll be waiting with the case.'

The collection of his case took place as expected and without incident as usual, and for the first time that day, Dirk felt like he was able to relax, he finished the champagne and retired to bed. He slept undisturbed for 15 hours.

Chapter 3

Paul had spent almost all of yesterday afternoon on the phone and had managed to arrange both the tasks given to his care by De Cathay and Brazi. The first had been relatively easy. He had known Roger Barlow for over 20 years. A close family friend, also from Yorkshire who had moved away to run a small bar just off the red-light area in Amsterdam. An ex policeman and part time private investigator, Paul had often used his 'other services', guaranteed absolute discretion, as this work clearly required. Roger had in fact been incredibly useful for Paul over the years, arranging contacts for the girls he regularly employed on behalf of De Cathay as well as providing good quality, discounted cannabis, probably Pauls only vice. Roger knew the Neerdorf estate well having supplied a couple of girls for parties hosted by the elder twin son, Erik. He had also supplied Mrs Neerdorf with her special cigarettes when her husband was away out of town. Co-incidentally, he'd received a call that very day from her and was due to deliver later that evening. Paul mentally ticked off that, that particular task would be an easy one, and he knew the Vatican business records were accurate, it would do no harm however to get pictorial proof as well and of course, for the right price, Roger accepted the work.

The second task was obviously going to take a lot more thought and planning. Paul knew the German couple were capable of seeing the task through and what's more they were available. They were at present laying low after the last successful job Paul has tasked them with. Anita had demonstrated once more, her uncompromising professionalism in manufacturing the accidental death of a Syrian diplomat and Gert used his highly competent skills to locate and recover the ancient early Christian scrolls, said to be the work of Judas Iscariot. The Syrian was in Malta to sell them to the church for an appropriate fee, agreed in the days earlier with The Vatican hierarchy. Paul had been delighted to deliver this hugely important record that detailed in Hebrew text the weeks leading up to the betrayal of Christ. Even more so that it cost just a fraction of the $10m price tag. Strange how things work out he thought; he had taken a big risk in Malta, not sure if the couple could pull it off and then quickly disappear. As it happened, it had been a huge success, the Syrians didn't suspect what had really happened, they even apologised to Rome that their man had failed to deliver and what's more, they had lost the scrolls. De Cathay had performed particularly well during the conference call Paul thought, portraying his dismay by way of an enraged rebuttal whilst actually having the scrolls on the desk in front of him under a protective screen. It had in fact turned out to be the perfect test run for the couple ahead of this new sensitive assignment. He would pay the Germans from the proceeds of the recovery as well, so it was all very clean.

Paul contacted the couple at the safe house in Morocco, detailing the mission and agreeing a price. Tickets for travel and accommodation reserved and paid for, he was happy that within a couple of days the Vatican vaults would be replenished with whatever a 'significant amount of cash' was.

The phone on his desk rang and recognising the name displayed on its small screen he picked it up immediately to the press secretary of the Pope himself. Eduardo Musso was highly regarded, very charismatic and seemed to know everything about everything. Paul had asked him once, as a test, what he knew about the New Zealand economy expecting a bit of information about the volume of sheep on the islands. He got however over the next 20 mins an in-depth comprehensive report about the place, its people and financial standing. Musso was indeed a very impressive character of slight build, at just over 5ft 5in tall. He sported a bald dome of a head and a magnificent, greying full face beard.

'Paulo, how are you, I need to talk with you if I may, just a very quick question....' Not a day for too many pleasantries Paul thought given the unusually direct greeting. Before Paul could respond Musso launched into dialogue again 'we have received a couple of media enquiries asking if his Holiness knows the whereabouts of the Judas scrolls. Remind me Paulo, how did we, you, acquire them again?'

Paul hesitated, jolted slightly by the question 'I thought we had decided not to make this find public Eduardo'

'Indeed Paulo, you are of course correct, and we will maintain that we don't know its whereabouts'

'So, what are you asking?'

'It seems that CNN are running a story tomorrow suggesting that the Vatican is connected with an incident in Malta...'

'How preposterous' Paul interjected with as much indignation as he could muster

'Yes, it is Paulo, but I am troubled. I can see from the expenses ledger that we had people in Valetta on the day in question'

'Eduardo, I am Head of Vatican Security, why would I know of these things?'

'Ah yes, why indeed. It is a question that is asked often around here Paulo'

'Look, sorry I have no knowledge of anything in Malta or anywhere else, neither do I have any idea how the acquisition processes of other Vatican departments work'

There was a short silence, Paul could here Eduardo breathing heavily on the other side of the phone.

'Be warned Paulo, don't let this come back to you, His Holiness will not be pleased. The phone went dead, Paul took a deep breath and cursed himself. How stupid he had been to put his lunch on expenses that day and how worrying that Eduardo Musso wasn't one of the names in his little black book of indiscretions.

As he sat down there was a knock on his door, it opened immediately before Paul could respond. De Cathay entered, demonstrating the perception of him being big, loud and rude. As the door swung closed, Georges huge cassock flapped wildly in the rush for him to get inside. 'Any news Paulo?' his voice warm and friendly, arms outstretched as though welcoming an old friend.

'Hi, come in Georges' the sarcasm missed its mark on the Frenchman 'I'm happy to report that both items on the to-do list are being attended to as we speak'

'Excellent, I never doubted that would be the case, and, have you managed to keep up to date with your usual schedule?'

Paul smiled, knowing which part of his usual schedule was being referred to 'all in order yes. I think you will be especially pleased this week, we have an old favourite returning.'

'Fantastic, its good to see you on top form. Everything else ok?'

Paul gave thought for a second 'well, as you ask. I think we may have a problem with Eduardo, he is asking questions about Malta'

Georges stopped momentarily, 'I heard he was fending off some hacks from the US press, he doesn't know anything so don't worry and he has instructions from his boss to just follow the company line.'

'Yes, but he worries me, he only stops when he's satisfied his curiosity, it what he does.'

'Paulo, don't spend time thinking about Musso, if he becomes a problem for you, I'll speak with him'

Conversation over, De Cathay moved towards the door and then hesitated. Turning he looked at Paul 'we need to give some thought to Alberto; he is our weak link and I fear he may cause us problems. Give it some thought Paulo'. Before Paul could respond, Georges was gone as quickly as he had arrived. Paul sat and considered things for a while, in particular the fate of Signor Brazi. Aside from that, all was in fact in order and going as planned, he was delivering everything he'd been asked to. Nonetheless, he couldn't get the conversation with Musso out of his head and it did bother him. Paul had taken delivery of the scrolls himself in Malta and left a trail. A fundamental some would say, schoolboy error and one he hoped wouldn't come back and hurt him. Having said that, he had been congratulated for the work, the letter he had proudly received, signed by the Pontiff himself was proof of that. If only he knew what went on his name Paul mussed. The people around him work very hard to keep the boss pure.

Paul's mobile pinged the arrival of a new text message. He smiled as he read that the German couple were on holiday in Kos and had spotted their quarry arrive, they were keeping an eye on his movements.

The smile grew into a broad grin as he realised that the pictures attached to an email from rbarlow.work@hotmail.com opened showing a nice family gathering of a mother and her two sons. Task 1 completed, and the return email confirmed payment would be made in the usual manner, within the hour.

Chapter 4

Over the past couple of days, the quiet unassuming German couple had observed Neerdorf arrive for breakfast at 8am prompt where he took a single boiled egg, two pieces of wholemeal toast cut straight off the loaf and a single cup of freshly brewed coffee, no milk or sugar, finished it off. Lunch was at 1:15pm and consisted of something from the salad bar. He left his apartment at 6:30pm every evening to meet with different people but at the same restaurant; Giadji in nearby Kardemina. It was nicely positioned, and he had a reserved table looking out at the small fishing harbour where he took a large bowl of mussels and a cold jug of house white wine. The large mussels were in fact Dirk's favourite, the Mariniere sauce at this particular restaurant was the best he had ever eaten anywhere in the world and the service was always good. In between lunch and dinner, he took a swim at 4pm, 32 lengths in just about half an hour. It was these 30 minutes that the Germans would use today to undertake their work.

Gert had already secured a master key. The cleaners in this complex were no different than anywhere else. The hotel rule was that keys were locked in the communal staff safe at the end of each shift. They were supposed to be signed in and out by the supervising member but that hardly ever happened. The cleaners and maintenance staff who used it, assumed that the hotel guests didn't even know the staff room existed, so what security risk was there!?

At 4:05 Dirk was starting his second length in the pool, start slowly finish with a flourish was how he liked it. At the same time Anita was entering his room and Gert was in a taxi heading to the secure vaults located in Kos town. The day before Gert had completed a thorough search of the apartment knowing that it was highly unlikely that the large case described by Hindle would still be there. He was of course correct but had found the deposit room instructions on Neerdorf's briefcase. Astonished at the amount involved, he had been able to organise a scanned copy and replace the original with just a minute to spare before Dirk had returned to the room.

Anita knew the layout of the spacious apartment in minute detail. She knew the minibar, which was stocked with still water, a chilling bottle of Sancerre and two half bottles of Veuve Clicquot was next to the slatted louvre doors leading onto the balcony. Beyond that, was the concrete wall that Neerdorf would be stood next to, glass in hand, admiring the shimmering blue vista. The wall was a little under 3 feet high, just below her target's waistline. She had prepared a lure earlier in the day using a photo of Neerdorf's wife that Gert had removed the day before. It was now flapping in the breeze off the wall, secured by some wire. Anita's riskiest decision was yet to be made; which hiding place to adopt of the three that she had identified. The curtain was too risky, it afforded little view of the balcony and was too near to the fridge. The wardrobes offered the best protection but still posed a risk in that they were across the room. Opening the heavy doors of the wardrobe she found that true to form, they were organised in perfect order. Formal suits and trousers with appropriate shoes in one, casual shirts, slacks and deck shoes in the other. It was an easy gamble that if he intended to leave for dinner at 6:30pm he would go for Chino's and a short-sleeved oxford shirt, so Anita cleared a small space in the formal wardrobe and waited. She had the insurance of a kitchen knife secured in the leg of her brown boot in case she was discovered but, she trusted her instinct, hoping that the messy option wouldn't be necessary. It was dark, hot and uncomfortable, the only light coming in from the small opening between the two doors that would allow her to view Neerdorf and execute her plan. It was difficult for her to get her breath, which wasn't unusual in this circumstance, she had to bring her heart rate down so consciously took deeper, slower and quieter breaths forcing the oxygen into her body and relaxing as much as she dared. Dirk entered the room finishing off a conversation on the phone, confirming his dinner appointment at Giadji. He'd leave at 6:30pm and get a cab. His key entered the power slot on the wall just inside the door, the aircon immediately burst into life and the light in the bathroom illuminated the apartment. He'd obviously uncharacteristically left it on when he left earlier, he thought about it fleetingly convincing himself that he must have been in more of a rush than he'd realised.

Anita watched silently as Neerdorf broke the seal on the cold bottle and poured a glass of white wine, at the same time opening the balcony door. He sensed immediately that something was wrong, he knew someone had been in the room. There was a faint odour of an unfamiliar scent in the air, the notebook and pen on the table had been moved. He looked around slightly unnerved and seeing one of his shoes had fallen out of the formal wardrobe. Moving to the phone at the side of the bed, he was about to call reception to complain when something on the balcony caught his eye. It looked like a photograph, flapping against the breeze on the balcony wall but, how could that be. What the hell was going on? Dirk slipped out onto the balcony and peered over the edge. Puzzled at the picture of his wife blowing about on what seemed to be a wire stuck to the stonework, he leaned over and took the wire in his hand trying to figure out what was securing it. The force of the push stung his back and buttocks but that was nothing compared to the fear that struck him as he realised, he was falling headfirst onto the rocks 30 feet below. In the few seconds it took for Dirk to smash into the sharp edges of the white and grey boulders that edged the lapping ripples of the Aegean, the momentum of the push had rolled his body, so he was twisting as he fell. Strangely he felt no pain as his collar bone, ribs, left arm and leg gave way under the force of the impact. As consciousness ebbed away, he wondered if the ghostly apparition of a female form looking down at him, was in fact an angel. The last thing he remembered was the smash of his wine glass on the rocks a few feet away, but he was sure he had put the glass down on the table. He felt his eyes heavy; he knew his body was twisted and broken, then emptiness, a darkness ensued, and he knew nothing more.

Very happy with the fact that all had gone to plan, Anita tossed the glass of wine after Neerdorf. Someone might assume he'd been a little disorientated in the hot sun. She recovered the photograph and placed it carefully back where Gert had said he'd found it and swiftly exited the apartment. She could already hear a distant siren as she took off the surgical gloves that she favoured for this type of operation and placed them in a bin in the corridor. The lift doors opened to three men in hotel attire running, panicked towards the room she had just vacated. With two small bags already packed, check out was swift and easy and the waiting taxi took just 20 minutes to get her to the airport and a rendezvous with her partner.

Chapter 5

Gert arrived at the vaults and paid the taxi driver. He decided not to ask the bad tempered, unshaven driver to wait having noted that there were plenty of plated silver Mercedes for hire within a few yards of where he was. Having read and memorised the access instructions, Gert approached the unmarked, anonymous building and entered the 5-digit code into the keypad. The lock gave a reassuring click and he entered the lobby looking every inch like a city financier. The lobby was huge, circular and empty except for a large, dark mirrored wall which obviously hid a monitoring station where four CCTV cameras recorded every angle of any activity that stirred on the floor. To the left of the mirror, positioned in a semi-circle were six numbered doors, each with its own keypad and intercom. Gert confidently approached door 5 and pressed the intercom buzzer. It was silent for a moment but then his presence was acknowledged by a small red light above the number pad, a human voice in perfect English said 'welcome to operator number 5 please identify yourself ' Gert again entered the same 5 digit number into the keypad 'Thank you ' The warmth of the soft female voice was reassuring 'Enter please' Door number 5 opened quietly and Gert walked through it into a high walled chamber. The door Behind him closed shut. A different voice this time, automated, mechanical, echoed into the room 'Enter your security code and speak your ID clearly please' Gert noticed the cold from the air con unit blowing from the ceiling, realising whilst looking around that if this went wrong he would have no means of escape. His slight panic was short lived, and he continued to the walled iPad in front of him. Only 3 digits this time resulting in a white light appearing on the wall, he spoke clearly and confidently into the circular grill 'Neerdorf Securities limited, agent 002' He waited for a few seconds in silence, the automated voice cackled and startled him slightly 'Thank you Mr Neerdorf, Enter your code again please and speak your ID into the intercom'

Gert repeated the process not sure if this was usual, he started to feel anxious.

'Thank you, Mr Neerdorf, your assistant will be with you shortly'. He relaxed breathing a sigh of relief, but even though the room was cold he felt the sweat run down the side of his face. He wiped it with a tissue as a hatch slid open in the wall next to the intercom. He hadn't even seen the join so was surprised to see the sliding panel which opened onto a glass pane, behind which set the smiling face of a young man whose name badge identified him as Kristos. 'Good afternoon sir and welcome back to Culis vaults, do you have your release document please?' Gert posted the stolen piece of A4 paper through a dispenser slot under the glass. The sheet of paper was headed Cullis Vaults and had a watermark through it depicting a castle portcullis and the words 'Cavendo Tutus'. The release instructions he'd recovered from the apartment had been followed to the letter and Gert felt relatively comfortable.

'This is all in order Mr Neerdorf, I will sign off your request and you can collect your case through the door on your left in just a few minutes'. A slide panel moved revealing another doorway and another room.' Thank you for using Cullis Vaults sir, we hope to see you again soon'.

A huge sense of relief passed through Gert's body, 5 minutes and he would be back in a taxi heading for Kos airport. He entered the room and instinctively took a seat waiting for delivery of the case.

The door behind him closed and there was silence. Unconcerned he thought about the safe house and a month in Rio de Janeiro with his compatriot and the 100,000 Euro's that would by now be sitting in the office account. The sound of the Englishman's voice shook him back to reality 'Good afternoon Sir, would you mind identifying yourself please?'

'Again' thought Gert, red tape and rules to be followed he assumed. He could not see any keypad or intercom so decided to speak out loud the numbered code and ID 'Neerdorf securities limited' His voice echoed in the chamber 'agent zero, zero two'.

'No!' the voice came back, methodical, superior, 'your real name please'

Gert thought hard for a few moments, not sure how to respond. He had followed the instructions, passed through each phase of the security process.

'your real name, if you don't mind' the voice repeated itself 'it might help if I tell you that the room you are in is secure, you are being recorded and you will not be leaving here with the item you seek'

Gert slumped into his seat realising he was never going to have completed this part of the mission successfully. How foolish to think he could just stroll up to the vault and walk away with $5m. He was trapped, however he mused, he wasn't yet caught.

The Englishman troubled him slightly, the British were always very thorough, extremely careful but he was still in Greece. He comforted himself that there would be plenty of opportunity to buy his way out of this mess. Gert had decided to say nothing more and in the last half hour he'd learned that Neerdorf senior had met his fate and his son, the only other person able to make this collection was still in Holland, probably unaware of any problems. The blind interrogation continued but it was easy for Gert to just sit and say nothing. It could only be a matter of time before the Greek police came and arrested him, that would be his chance to walk free.

Chapter 6

Paul's second mobile rattled in his desk drawer as it buzzed silently. He looked alarmed as he opened his draw and recognised the name on the display 'Anita, is everything ok?'

'My work is complete, but my friend hasn't arrived at the airport, they are making the final call'

Paul's mind raced over the scenario's that might lead to the normally efficient German missing a flight. 'ok, let it go without you' Hindle always had a plan B, the small cost of obtaining alternative flights always provided insurance and assurance against a host of eventualities 'there's a flight to London via Rome boarding in two hours, tickets and passes are waiting for you in a safety deposit box at the airport' Hindle continued to give the details and wished her well 'whatever happens, be on that one and you will be met at Heathrow with tickets for the connection to Rio'

Anita was concerned, her partner had never let her down in all the time they had worked together and she knew instinctively that there was a problem. She prayed that Hindle could sort it out.

Paul put his phone back in the drawer and immediately dialled Rome's Chief of Police from his landline. 10 minutes later, Paul left his office feeling marginally better and hopeful that his good friend at the Police department would provide the solution to both of his immediate problems.

Gert sat poker faced, staring at the wall. The questions had stopped, and Gert realised that the heat he felt was natural and not enhanced by the stress of his situation. The room he sat in was almost eerie, it was deadly silent, dimly lit and getting increasingly uncomfortable as the air conditioning had stopped or had been turned off. As he sat and contemplated his fate, he heard an occasional electrical cackle over the speaker system, no spoken words but clearly someone was there quietly listening, waiting for him to break his own silence, he remained steadfast but was feeling weary as the temperature rose higher.

A screen opened in the wall and a human face peered out from behind the thick glass. Gert looked and tried to bring the image into focus. As it did, he realised that the man staring at him was in police uniform and was attended by another uniformed officer and an agitated gentleman in a grey suit, white shirt and striking red tie. The three were engaged in what looked like a heated conversation, all three clearly debating Gert's fate and worryingly, there was conflict. After what seemed like an age, the suited gent took a call on his mobile that lasted less than a minute. During that time, he said nothing, just listened, and as he put the mobile phone back in his pocket a door opened in the chamber and the two policemen appeared. Gert instinctively got to his feet and as he saw the handcuffs, offered his wrists. The metal clasp clicked securely, and he was led out of the chamber and through a circular corridor. They were alone, it was quiet, and no-one spoke until they came to a stop at a flight of stairs. The senior of the two police officers turned and looked at him directly, staring him in the eye, unblinking and cold. He placed a hood over his head; 'at the bottom of these stairs, we will exit this building and enter a waiting vehicle. Once in the vehicle, you will sit still and say nothing; as we exit the door before you get into our waiting vehicle, you will look at the floor, do not under any circumstances attempt any form of communication and do not attempt to remove this hood. It is all that lay between your freedom and 20 years hard labour in prison.' Gert felt a hand on his shoulder and another on his arm, he was led down fifteen steps and out onto a concrete floor. He heard what sounded like a van door slide open and then lost balance as he was pushed forwards, stumbling he fell onto what felt like a bench seat. 'Stay still and flat', the door slammed shut and the engine purred into life before moving off, slowly at first, then at considerable speed. The journey was alarmingly uncomfortable and no matter how hard he tried, he just couldn't remain still, falling off the seat as the vehicle rounded a particularly sharp bend. The words he had heard a few minutes earlier were running around his head in short snippets as Gert tried to make sense with what was happening, particularly the bit about his freedom, what did that mean? The vehicle screeched to a stop and he heard the door open. He was pulled out onto a grass roadside verge and the hood was removed. The sunlight hit his eyes and it took him a minute to regain focus. During that time, he was able to establish that the vehicle he'd been travelling in was in fact a dirty white police mini bus, the windows were blacked out and the blue lights were whirling. As he came to his senses, the minibus sped off and left him stood next to a heavy set, police officer, older in appearance that the two who had collected him earlier. The uniform suggested a very senior rank and the craggy lined face hinted at many years' experience 'Hello' he smiled 'you probably have many questions but I would urge you to keep them to yourself, we have little time and you have a long journey ahead' Gert looked at his attendant quizzically but said nothing. 'come, my car awaits, please get in the back and don't forget your seat-belt' Gert followed the instruction and got into the rear of the Mercedes, noticing as he did a driver already in place and the engine running. The police officer got in from the other door and sat alongside him. 'to the airport driver please, as quick as you can'. Gert's heart missed a beat as he realised he was going to be let free. He turned to the other passenger 'what is happening here?' he asked

'You have no need to be concerned Gert' his name was used for the first time 'just be thankful that you have some very powerful friends'. He handed Gert an envelope 'You have a fast-track ticket for the next plane to Rome and a connecting flight to London Heathrow. Take it and move quickly through the onboarding process, you will not be hindered, and you will find your companion on the plane.'

The car came to a stop at the departures gate and all three people got out. The driver opened the boot and took out a suitcase and a smaller brief case. He recognised the suitcase, it was Gert's pre-packed baggage from the hotel, the other he hadn't seen before but both were handed over to the German. 'Have a pleasant trip sir' he said. The officer turned to get back in the car, he hesitated before doing so and addressed Gert 'don't be in a rush to return to Greece' he looked at the driver 'can you place my briefcase in the boot please and then get me back to HQ' The driver complied and the car set off as Gert entered the airport clutching his travel baggage and a briefcase full of more money than he had ever laid eyes on, he started his journey to freedom.

Chapter 7

4 Hours later at Culis Vaults.

The intercom burst into life 'hello how can we help you?'
'I am trying to gain entry to the lobby, but the keypad doesn't recognise my security code'
'Stand directly in front of the camera please'
The camera buzzed and a door opened 'please enter, we will attend to you shortly'
He entered a small room that had a seat, table and drinking water cooler in it. The seat faced a window behind which sat a middle-aged man in suit and tie. 'How can we help you today?'
'My father deposited an amount of cash here a few days ago, he's been involved in an unfortunate accident, so I am here on his behalf to retrieve the money. My security details however aren't being recognised'
'Let me take the details and check for you sir'
Thomas Neerdorf passed the security details through a post slot in the wall and waited. After half an hour the attendant returned.
'I'm sorry to say Mr Neerdorf, we don't have any record of receiving any deposit from your father and the security details you provided here relate to a transaction from last year, not in your name'
Thomas stood dumbfounded 'but you must have, he was here a few days ago, check your CCTV systems, look at the transactional record for our account'
'We have checked Mr Neerdorf, there must be some confusion on your part here. Our systems have no record of your father attending this facility in the last 3 months, your transactional record does not contain any activity in that time also. Mr Neerdorf, your bank has not deposited any money here for quite some time and your account with us rests at a zero balance.'
'That can't be true, I want to see someone more senior….'
The door behind him opened 'goodbye sir, thanks for visiting us today'

Rome Leonardo Da Vinci airport

Paul saw the arrival from Kos land, from his seat in the lounge area. He watched satisfied as Gert and the briefcase walked off the plane and he relaxed as the case was handed over to his PA in the meeting area. The two people parted company quickly and without speaking any words to each other.

6 Hours later…London Heathrow airport.

No-one gave the two weary looking German tourists a second glance. Their luggage passed through check-in, passports viewed and cleared and off they went through the control area onto the concourse and into the Boeing 747, taking their seats and getting settled for the flight to Rio. Eight rows back, a genteel looking man in black robe and dog collar, pressed send on his text message 'the couple are going on holiday'.

Vatican City

Paul had been summoned to the office of Georges De-Cathay where he found the imposing frame of his colleague sat menacingly behind the familiar old oak desk. Sat next to him a frail looking Brazi, both looked at him as he entered the room and as he acknowledged them, Paul saw both extremes of the human state, being scared of one and fearful for the other.

'Paul, welcome. What news have you regarding your recent assignment?' enquired De Cathay

'it is good Georges, all is well, and our bank account shows that an hour ago, $5m was deposited into it'

De-Cathay's demeanour changed immediately as a broad smile spread across his face and he held his arms open wide 'I knew you'd never let us down Paul, what about the banker?'

'He is in a….better place, we won't be hearing from him any time soon. Like I said, all is well and there is no trail for anyone to follow'

'Come, have a small drink to celebrate' De Cathay opened a cabinet and removed a bottle of fine cognac and three glasses

'No thank you, I have to be somewhere Georges' Paul moved to the door 'Alberto?'

Brazi looked at Paul thankfully, 'yes me too, I have an appointment' he rose and made to the door.

'ok as you wish' said Georges 'come back when you have time and we'll take our toast'

The two men exited and walked swiftly down the corridor. Paul turned to address Brazi just as the priest fell to his knees, holding his chest, gasping for breath, the pain soaring through his body etched on his ashen white face. Paul rushed to support his friend as he struggled to speak through short, rasping breaths, 'Paulo, I…need to…attend…confession, can you…hear me please'. Paul held his friend and colleague, struggling to comprehend what was happening, he grasped his hand, it was cold and clammy, Alberto's whole body was shaking, his eyes were bulging. Paul looked around for help, but the corridors remained silent, every large solid ancient door was closed. Sunlight streamed through the high windows casting long lines of almost angelic bright white light onto the tiled floors. Paul held his breath and closed his eyes, placing his hand over Alberto's mouth and nostrils, he held firm until he felt the body he was supporting go limp. There was no struggle, he was much too weak for that. After just a few more seconds during which he sought God's forgiveness, Paul gently lay the lifeless form onto the ground, closing the eyelids to cover the alarmed, frightened, bulging, red eyes.

'Rest in peace my friend, rest in peace…'

Chapter 8

After 3 months of drifting in and out of consciousness, corrective surgery, excruciating pain, and various therapies designed to bring back his speech and mobility, Dirk Neerdorf was demanding to be discharged from his small, personal room in the private hospital that had been his prison since that awful incident at the hotel in Kos. After falling from the balcony of his hotel room onto the sandstone boulders below, his nightmare had only just begun. He had broken nearly every bone down the left-hand side of his body, punctured a lung, fractured his skull, and suffered a huge bleed on his brain. The emergency services attending were convinced he wouldn't make it to the hospital, such was the extent of his appalling injuries and it is testament to their expertise that he made it. He had to be resuscitated twice in the ambulance after he had stopped breathing, the paramedics had skilfully and successfully worked on his broken form throughout the 30 minute journey to the emergency room at the hospital some 20 miles away where he was quickly transferred to the operating theatre for 19 hours under the care of the surgeon and a team of specialists. Whilst in theatre the heart monitor flat lined another two times as the medics fought hard to keep him alive with an artificial heart pump, drugs, and sophisticated electronic machinery, until eventually, in a drug induced coma, Dirk was released from theatre to an isolation care room where he was given 24-hour constant attention and a police guard.

Chapter 9

3 months earlier

Back at the hotel the local police were still in attendance and trying to piece together the events that had led to the highly respected businessman falling from his bedroom window in broad daylight. It had been thought that maybe, he had taken a bit too much wine, but the fact that the half bottle was open and had most of its contents still present put paid to that theory. That and CCTV had picked him up walking back to his room after a swim in the pool suggested that drunkenness didn't play a part in this scenario. The hotel room was closed off so the police could complete a full, detailed forensic review but they found nothing of any value to their investigation. They did see that one of the wardrobes was untidy and a jacket had fallen off its hanger onto the shoes but that didn't create any concern; they found a picture of Mrs Neerdorf on the table top but that was to be expected, especially for a man like Dirk who clearly loved his wife dearly and would have missed her when he was away on business. After 24 hours, during which the hotel manager had complained many times about requiring the room back for guests, the police could find nothing untoward that might explain some foul play or outside interference. In any event, according to the duty manager, access to the rooms was impossible for anyone other than cleaning staff and the paying occupant of the specific room. All room keys were subject to rigorous discipline and any member of staff found not to comply would be in danger of immediate disciplinary action including dismissal. Roman Targ was the police chief in charge of this investigation. He was in his mid-fifties with thirty years' service under his belt. He knew instinctively that there was nothing to be found here and that the Dutch man had for whatever reason, lost balance and just fallen over the edge of the balcony. He knew also, that if he found that not to be true, the paperwork attached to the case and the hours of working on it would escalate into weeks, possibly months of long days and late nights. It suited him and indeed his team if this matter was brought to a close as soon as possible and he was careful to make sure that all the necessary boxes had been ticked, nothing had been found, and the desk-top template report was almost complete. He could probably be home with a few beers, before AEK Athens kick-off their Super league 1 game that evening. AEK was his team and always had been since he was a boy at school. He could play himself in those days; his well-built frame and strong aggressive attitude made him well sought after as a mid-fielder but as the years passed and his lack of real ability became apparent, he settled for just watching. He still loved the game though and watched as much as he could fit into his schedule. Even the local Kos team who were a non-league outfit these days were good to watch occasionally. As Targ did a last survey of the room, mentally noting the surroundings he remembered that he didn't have a statement from any of the cleaning or maintenance staff. He thought for a while and decided to delegate the duty to one of the young detectives knowing that a delay of another hour would make him late for kick-off. Alexis Demetriou was new to the team having been plucked from the local front-line officers after being identified as ambitious with a great attention to detail. He was keen to get ahead and relished every opportunity to get involved and serve the community.

Roman popped his head around the apartment door 'Alexis' he shouted down the hallway towards the young detective 'I have a job for you'

Alexis immediately responded, bounding towards the room like an obedient Labrador, always keen to impress his superiors 'yes sir' he answered, 'what can I do to help?'

Targ watched unimpressed, his overweight frame sagging in his sweaty shirt and jacket, 'I know we've spoken with the maintenance staff, but I don't appear to have any supporting documentation to go with the end report. We need to quickly box it off please, just get a statement from the supervisor if you can, it just needs to say they saw and heard nothing and importantly, that the keys were not compromised. Understand?'

'yes sir, leave that with me, I'll have it back to you this evening'

'tomorrow Demetriou, I don't want to see it until tomorrow' Targ smirked and left the youngster to his thoughts.

In the isolation ward at the hospital, Dirk was still in an induced coma. His wife had arranged and paid for a dedicated nurse so that the patient was with someone constantly. The hospital had of course, placed a group of specialist nurses on a rota to cover each day and ensure that when Dirk came round, he would be immediately tended to and an alert could be sent to his family who were on route to Kos to join Thomas who had arrived on the day of the incident. He was already at that time, worried that his father might be in danger after a phone conversation earlier in the day where he detected enough vagueness in his fathers' account to make him stop what he was doing and make the journey to Kos to help the company CEO. The problem he was struggling with was that they had been discussing an issue with the Catholic Church who had defaulted on a loan repayment. The incident with his father must surely be a coincidence, it was inconceivable that the Vatican could be even remotely involved in the attempted murder of one of its key business partners. But he just couldn't get it from his mind.

At that moment the phone rang, Thomas looked at the display and answered in immediately 'Erik, how are you getting on?'

'its slow, hot and frustrating, we'll be in Kos tomorrow by the looks of things, we've organised a locum pilot, but he can only get to Amsterdam in the morning. Our jet is ready though and we have clearance sorted to land in Athens mid-morning. I've arranged for us to be met at the airport and a taxi boat will bring us straight to the island so with any luck, we'll be with you by noon. How are you anyway, what's the latest?'

Thomas thought carefully for a few seconds, he didn't want to unduly worry his brother, or his mother come to that, but he had to be straight 'listen, Erik, I don't know what's going on here. Dad is alive and safe; he's got constant attention and a guard on the door. I'm just going back to the Vaults to confirm that the money has been banked and then I'll go back to my apartment and get some rest before you and mum arrive. I don't get it though Erik, he wasn't drunk and there is no way he'd have just fallen from a hotel balcony…'

'what are the police saying Thomas?'

'nothing much at the moment but it is early days. They are on site and undertaking a thorough investigation'

'Thorough? They don't know what that means Thomas, we need to keep close to them and keep them on their toes'

'ok Erik, we can do that together tomorrow. I've rented a villa for us to use as a base, I'll send you the address. It seemed a better option than using a hotel where we would be more visible and exposed.'

The words hit Erik hard 'what? You think we might be targets? I won't be bringing mum if you think that Thomas'

'No, sorry' Thomas scolded himself for speaking without thinking 'wrong use of words, I mean, it'll be a more comfortable environment to go about our business'

'ok, if you say so. I'm not taking any risks…'

'Yes, I understand and agree. Erik, my taxi has just arrived, so I'll speak with you in the morning. Stay safe brother and look after mum'

The phone went dead before Erik could respond, he sat for a second mulling it all over in his mind, 'are we really targets for an unknown murderer and why does Thomas need to confirm that the money was banked, dad had confirmed that already…'

Chapter 10

Alexis walked down into the hotel basement in the hope of finding the duty supervisor but there was no-one about. 'hello, anyone here' Alexis questioned the room. He heard a movement beyond the main door and walked over, entering and looking around he caught a glimpse of a figure in a curtained cubicle 'hello, anyone in here? It's the police' There was a bump as the figure behind the curtain fell into the adjoining wall 'shit! How can anyone get changed in here, these cubicles are just too small'

'hello?' Alexis raised his voice

'who the fuck is it, what do you want? I'm getting bloody changed for Christ's sake…'

'I'm detective Demetriou I just need to ask you a few questions'

'well fuck off, I'm busy. I talked to you lot earlier, you know all that I know and that's fuck all'

'I'm sorry sir, I just need to get a statement I can wait for you' Alexis sat down on one of the bench seats in the staff changing room. The curtain pulled back and a slight older man walked out, dressed in dirty jeans and white t-shirt. His unshaven, wrinkled face glanced over at Alexis 'still here?'

'I'm sorry to bother you again sir, I'll only be a few minutes, I just need to finish the paperwork off. What's your name?'

'My name? Why? I just told you I don't know anything'

'I just need to view the key cabinet?'

'what about it? Its over there' the man pointed a long scaly finger towards a tall steel cabinet in the corner of the room. It was slim and a dull steel grey colour. What looked like a new combination style lock secured it and its feet were bolted into the concrete floor. It looked to Alexis as though it was secure enough. 'who has access to the lock?' he asked

The man shuffled his feet and hunched his shoulders 'just the staff. Cleaners and maintenance only, and the managers of course. No-one else knows the combination number' he moved towards the door and Alexis jumped up quickly to block his way 'wait, not so fast. Your name please' He stood between the man and the door, facing him head on and making it clear he wasn't going anywhere

'for fuck sake. Gregor Illianov, I'm an exile from Lithuania. I've been in Greece for 15 years and never had any trouble. I just want to be left alone; I don't want no-one knowing I'm here…'

'ok ok, I get it' said Alexis 'just a brief statement and you won't hear from us again, I promise. All I need is for you to open the cabinet, show me its locked properly, and then sign this statement I've completed. It just says that all is in order and nothing was out of place when the err incident happened'

Gregor turned and moved slowly to the cabinet, taking a piece of paper from his pocket he studied it for a second and then opened the combination lock, swinging the door open to reveal a wall of keys and passes. 'There, is that all?'

'you have the code written down?' Alexis enquired

'yes, I'm getting old, I can't remember so much stuff these days. Is that all?' Gregor closed the door and secured the lock. 'now, what else would you have me do?'

'just sign this statement please' Alexis handed over a hand-written document clipped to a board. Gregor read the first paragraph, all looked ok. It was standard stuff. 'There you go, can I leave now?'

Alexis took the document back and stood aside 'thank you Gregor, that is a great help'
Gregor sniffed and shuffled out of the door, coughing as he went.

Alexis read the statement he had just written, sat down on the bench and went over the detail again. Had he collected all the information that Targ would need to complete his reporting. He pondered for a few minutes.

'He's lying' the words entered the room and made Alexis jump with a start. He looked up and scanned the room just as a curtain in the far corner, diagonally opposite the key cabinet, pulled back and a short slender woman with tied up dark hair stepped out. She was dressed in a hotel overall and looked tired as though she had been working all day and night. 'good god woman, who are you and what are you doing in there?' Alexis jumped up rather annoyed
'he was lying to you, Gregor the Lithuanian, he knows what happened yesterday with the keys, it's he who bought the new lock this morning'
'what? You better explain what you mean, start with your name please'
'Gina Spiros, I am part of the maintenance team here at the hotel. I am here a lot, work as much as I can as I need the money and I see everything that goes on. The stealing from the stores, the affairs with the staff, the thefts from guests' rooms, everything...'
'ok then Gina, in what way was Gregor lying to me?'
'he and I were here the day before yesterday when a guy came into here and took one of the master keys. We both saw it happen...'
'what, hang on' Alexis interrupted 'just slow down a bit. So, you are saying that you saw some unauthorised person enter this changing area, open the cabinet and take a master room key? How can that happen?'
'it's easy, or it was easy until today. That cabinet was never locked, the rota log was never adhered to, no-one ever signed keys out or back in again. We told our supervisor what we had seen but by the time he got out of his office seat and came to see, the key was back'
'how long was that?'
'must have been about an hour, maybe a bit more. Hard to say really but we both went to find him, he was reluctant to come at first but then he wandered down, when the key was in its place, he didn't want to believe us. Then it all went mad yesterday and we find that the keys log has been filled in, back dated over the past few weeks, a new lock is bought and we are all given a new code and told to make sure we signed all keys in and out as well as storing our badges and ID cards properly. We saw him studying the CCTV late into the night, I suspect some of the coverage is missing...'
'what do you mean by that?'
'well that last thing he'll want is video of someone stealing access keys on his shift, so I'd guess he would have deleted it along with footage of him strolling down here to investigate.'
'so, what time of the day was that, when the keys were taken?'
'guessing, I'd say 12 maybe 12:30, just before lunch time'
Alexis stood, amazed and unclear. This was madness, the implications here were massive and changed the direction of this investigation immeasurably 'I need your address and phone number please, and if I can get an idea of your shift pattern that would be useful, I'll need to speak with you again over the next day or so. Where can I find your supervisors office?' he fired questions at her quickly and excitedly.
'it's up the stairs, first on the left. Please don't let on that I've given you any information, I need this job...'
'don't worry, we are discreet'.

Alexis, getting breathless with his heart starting to thump in his chest, left swiftly for the stairs and quickly found the first-floor office. A plaque on the door identified the Duty Supervisor's office and a slide plate confirmed that Andreas Papadopoulos was in situ. He knocked on the door and entered before Andreas could answer.

'Sorry to intrude' Alexis addressed Andreas as soon as he entered. 'I'm Alexis Demetriou, Detective...'

'more police, how many of you guys are there in this hotel? Have you not finished yet?'

'like I said, I'm sorry to intrude on your time I just have a few final things to cover off with you. I'm assuming you were on duty yesterday?'

'yeah, I've been here all week covering the day shift'

'good ok, I wonder if you can show me the CCTV system please'

'if you're looking for the tapes from yesterday, you lot already have them from the corridor covering the guys room, not that there is anything to see'

'what do you mean?'

'err, nothing. I just mean that when I looked at them with one of your colleagues, there was nothing out of order that we could see'

'and what about the day before, in the staff area, do you have coverage of that?'

'why would you want to see that?' Andreas noticeably stiffened 'that's just a staff area, its limited coverage as people get changed down there so its just the doorway really and its quite erratic'

'erratic?'

'well, it's not always switched on, we like to respect the privacy of our people'

'not very secure then, is that what you are saying?'

'that area is as secure as it needs er should be'

'well then, show me the recording of yesterday between 11:30am and 1:30pm please'

Andreas hesitated and a look of nervous tension appeared on his unshaven face 'it might take a while to set up...'

'let me see the system, I have experience of these things...' Alexis moved around the desk and hovered over Andreas' shoulder. 'I now this system well actually, it's a simple instruction...' he reached over and tapped the shift and esc keys then watching as a system menu popped up, he selected 'view, date/time'.

'I'm ok from here, leave it alone please' Andreas sounded annoyed as he moved Alexis's arms out of the way. Entering yesterday's date and the requested times he selected the staff area camera. It started to run a visual record of events from 11:30am. They both observed two members of staff enter and leave, both identified by Andreas as maintenance staff. No-one else entered or left in the next 15 minutes and the viewing screen went blank, as predicted. The time was 11:55am and the screen displayed an error message 'no video unavailable'. There was a block of unrecorded time that resumed at 2pm.

'So, what happed there then?' Alexis feigned surprise

'I did say it was a bit erratic, it sometimes switched itself off, especially if there is a long period of inactivity'

'but that is the time leading up to the lunch time, a new shift comes on during that time, surely it would have been recording'.

Andreas just looked up blankly and shrugged his shoulders 'I don't know, sorry...'

'can I see the keys log please, the one that signs keys in and out?'

'you guys already have it, your big boss took it yesterday, Targ I think his name is. Do you guys not speak with each other?' he smirked as he saw the anger rise in Alexis's face
'I'll be back later, what time do you go off shift today?'
'7pm today, it's a 12-hour day shift for me this week. What else could you want to know, you've asked everything now, at least four times between you all. Such a waste of tax-payers money…'
'save it' Alexis snapped 'I'm not happy with what I'm seeing and until I am, this whole hotel is a crime scene and me and my colleagues will come and go as we please' Alexis, getting a bit carried away with himself stopped and turned to leave 'it doesn't feel right and I'll carry on until I find what I'm looking for'. He left and descended the stairs out through the staff exit into the car park. Alexis sat in his car considering what he'd learned over the past hour and putting together in his mind how he would approach Targ with the information. Disconcerted he started the drive home to contemplate his next steps. Finally, he had an important case to work on, high visibility and potentially a career defining one that turns an accident file into an attempted murder. Happy, excited, he continued his short journey and envisioned his promotion at the end of the case and a fast track career progression up the ranks, it's what he's always wanted and had dreamed of since he was a boy. The phone rang and brought him back to earth, the number display showed Targ was calling, but he said leave it till tomorrow. The football was on tonight so for him to interrupt that must mean it's serious. 'Hello boss, is everything ok?'
'Demetriou, what have you been up to?
'up to sir?' Alexis snapped into alert mode, quickly realising the boss wasn't happy
'yes, UP TO? ' he shouted 'I've just had the regional commander on saying he's had a complaint from the hotel manager that my officers are harassing his already overworked and stressed staff. All I asked for from you was a closure document, THAT IS ALL!'
'but sir, I think I've uncovered something that makes this incident more sinister' Alexis spent the next 15 minutes going over what he had established
'Alexis, listen to yourself. You find some woman hiding in the staff room who reels off a wild tale of drama and you swallow it, hook, line and sinker. How likely does it all sound? Some mystery man steals a key the day before an accidental fall, and returns them after an hour of doing what? Even if that did happen, and it didn't, how can that be connected to something totally unrelated the day after?'
Alexis sat, listening to the tirade, deflated and almost crushed
'get that report on my desk first thing Alexis and I don't want to see any crap about conspiracies in it, do you get me?'
'yes sir' Alexis croaked. The phone went dead along with his dreams and the young detective drove home with welling tears of frustration in his eyes.
Targ picked up his phone for hopefully the last time this evening 'Good evening sir, I've spoken with my detective and you can inform your brother that our case is about to close on this matter and we won't be visiting his hotel again.'
'Very good and thank you Roman, it is very much appreciated. Tell me, how much attention did the Lithuanian get, I mean, is his identity secure?'
The question threw Targ for a second 'I don't think he was exposed in any way sir, why would you ask?'

'I'm interested only because I happen to know he's living under a protection order after helping Interpol some time ago, I'd hate his identity to be compromised and for there be repercussions on our island'

Targ remained silent, taking in the information that had just been shared and wondering whether there was a veiled threat in there somewhere 'I'll make sure there are no names in the reporting sir…'

'do better than that Roman, make sure that there is minimal reporting and no loose ends, I don't want any attention around this matter at all.' The Commander spoke with a calm but menacing tone and left Roman Targ in no doubt that he had just accepted another responsibility; to keep a previously hidden Lithuanian informant safe from harm.

'Fuck!' he cursed aloud and smashed his fist into the desk. He turned the volume up on his TV and opened another beer but from then and the rest of the night he just couldn't settle.

Chapter 11

The flight from Amsterdam arrived and landed on time at Athens International Airport, Spata. Erik and his mother remained on board whilst the authorities completed their customs checks and allowed for a quick re-fuel ahead of the short hop to Kos' local airfield. They had been offered the alternative to the planned ferry taxi by the airport after their pilot had filed the route plan and had taken it gratefully. It seemed that their private jet was small enough to use the local airstrip and the paperwork was very straight-forward.

The Mercedes GLB arrived at the pickup point and the uniformed driver immediately parked on the double yellow lines outside the departure hall. He had worked for the family before and the father in particular, so they knew each other well, Morgan was well known to the security team too and knew that he was safe leaving the car as he entered the hall to look for his employer. At 6ft3in he wasn't difficult to spot in a crowd, added to that his top heavy muscular frame, flat ears and misshaped nose from years of playing county level rugby union, he was given a wide berth by most passers-by which made his job a little easier and in this instance, collecting his passengers went very smoothly. 'Mrs Neerdorf, let me take those' he stooped and took both of her luggage bags, stopping to shake Erik's hand 'Hello sir, I hope you had a pleasant flight, I'm sorry it has to be under such bad circumstances'
'Thanks Morgan, it's good to see you again. How far have we got to walk to the car?'
'I'm just outside the door sir, it's just one minute' he smiled to himself knowing that his boss would be impressed and pleased. No-one else around here would be receiving the same service and he knew that Erik especially would revel in the admiring and not so admiring glances of the other people at the airport as he got into the back of the luxurious SUV and was swept away on the last leg of his journey. Morgan's close relationship with the Head of Security at the airport had its benefits although not everyone agreed, especially after they had announced their engagement earlier that year.
'I don't know how you do it Morgan, but this is a real blessing' Mrs Neerdorf smiled at the driver 'are we going to the hospital first?' she asked the question to either of the other two
'yes mother' Erik responded, 'father is still in a coma and so he won't be able to communicate with us, but I thought it best we see him before driving the short journey to the rented house organised by Thomas'.
Jumping into the brief silence Morgan offered 'I'm available for the duration of your stay Mr Neerdorf, so there is no time pressure'.
'excellent, and we're very grateful. Thank you so much.' Mrs Neerdorf was genuinely impressed with the driver so far, his rugged looks and easy charm helped as well.
The car slipped quietly across the town towards the private hospital ward. Morgan felt content that he had this job for at least a few weeks and his agreed day rate was more than he usually got in a week. He hadn't met the mother before but on first impressions, he was going to enjoy working for the family again. The investment he had made in the high end 4 x 4 with seven seats was perfect for a job like this, and he knew that the style and comfort the car provided his customers set him far and away above the competition that existed on this island. It certainly made him smile as he drove along around the towns and villages, as he watched the admiring and sometimes, jealous glances he attracted. He dropped his quarry at the hospital entrance and parked in a close by visitor's bay, leaving instructions with Erik to call him when they were ready to leave.

Deep inside the Vatican City walls Paul Hindle, Vatican Head of Security, was working quietly in his office, happy that recent events had improved the security and financial standing surrounding the church and its business concerns. There was still a significant debt to settle but the structure of the repayments was manageable, especially now that the church appeared to have some new flexibility around the terms and conditions attached to the draw down facility. Looking over the monthly update papers in detail and seeing that the current position had been downgraded on the risk register made him relax a little and he was pleased that the finance chief was now thinking about restructuring the deal on the back of what had transpired these last few days, to make it more equitable…for him. His desk phone startled him as it sprang into life. The display identified Eduardo Musso, Chief Press Secretary, as the caller and so this couldn't be a friendly catch-up call. Their previous encounters had been difficult to say the least, Musso's position made him very perceptive and by nature he was very direct, to the point of being aggressive, especially when he was on the scent of some wrong-doing or potential evolving scandal. Answering it nervously, Paul attempted to keep his voice strong and level 'Eduardo hello, what a pleasant surprise, what can I do for you today?'

Without returning pleasantries Musso sounded exasperated and tense 'what do you know about a finance firm called Neerdorf Securities, based in the Netherlands?'

There was a slight pause whilst Hindle quickly gathered his thoughts 'well, I do know that we have an arrangement with them, their CEO visited us recently, I met him briefly along with Cardinal Brazi and De Cathay'.

'yes, Senor Neerdorf. Did you know he is at this moment in a hospital on the island of Kos fighting for his life?'

Paul was under the impression that Neerdorf was dead, so this information threw him. 'I had no idea' he replied truthfully ' how serious is it and why is this information on your desk?' Paul could feel the heat rising in his face and a tension started to grip his body. He was sure that the German had reported that the mission was fully completed.

'It is reported that the man may not make it, but apparently he is a fighter and has the best physicians around him' He ignored the second question and waited for a response…

'This is indeed terrible news…' again being completely truthful.

'terrible yes,' interrupted Musso 'there is an alarming rumour circulating that the Catholic Church is involved in some way. I ask you again, what do you know?'

Hindle felt physically sick, he knew not to lie to or mislead Musso given his unnatural knack of knowing when those things were happening, but Hindle simply could not divulge all of what he knew.

'We have a financial arrangement with NS but it's all in order, up to date and is reported monthly in the Vatican corporate updates. The risk committee have a full view of it and in fact, they have downgraded the risk rating attached to the paper just this month.'

'All remarkably interesting but that isn't what I asked' Musso could sense the tension in his quarry's voice. 'Has anything, and I mean anything, happened to Dirk Neerdorf in the name of His Holiness, Paul?' the question was put across in a cold, menacing way that made the hairs on Paul's neck stand on edge and a shiver run through body.

'Eduardo, that is absolutely unthinkable and whoever is peddling those sorts of stories need to be held to account' Paul held his voice tone as well as he could but even he could sense the nervousness in it that might be about to betray him.

'yes, I understand that you are good at holding people to account' Musso responded quickly and with more than a hint of sarcasm. Changing the subject and his accusing tone, Musso reflected a little on the passing of his good friend Alberto Brazi. 'He was such a good man and represented us all perfectly. This place will miss him but I'm sure he will settle quickly in his new seat. It must have been a shock for you Paul, when he collapsed in front of you?' Paul felt it was more of a question than a statement 'yes incredibly sad, he passed quickly though and without suffering'.

'Actually, I think he suffered a lot, Paul' Musso retorted, his voice remaining cold and calm 'his last few months were difficult, and he seemed to be under a great deal of stress and pressure. The last time I saw him he appeared very troubled. Perhaps we'll never know why for sure. The surgeons have confirmed it was a massive heart attack now, so I'd guess he was just over-working'.

Paul remembered De Cathay telling him not to worry about the cause of death and any suspicion of it being unnatural, as one of his oldest friends and colleagues was Peter Manet, the Chief Medical Officer within the sacred walls. The post-mortem was to be conducted by Manet with Georges De Cathay looking over his shoulder.

Before Paul could respond Musso added 'at least I've identified a suitable successor'.

'Already?' questioned Hindle 'I was under the impression that Georges was leading the recruitment search?'

'I have a recommendation already, so the boss gave me permission to interview and appoint, as necessary. I can't say who it is yet as we've still to agree terms but this is a very strong person, younger than most of the dinosaurs around these parts and will be a breath of fresh air'.

Paul knew exactly what that meant, Musso had recruited someone who would be loyal to him and his position was about get even more powerful 'that's good news, I can't wait to meet him'.

Musso didn't respond. There was an uncomfortable silence that lasted just a few seconds but felt much longer, 'Paul, if the Church is implicated in any wrongdoing around Neerdorf, the Executive will take swift and direct action against those who are involved. I hope you understand'.

The phone went dead before Paul could respond. He sat in his chair and realised how fast his heart was beating, the beads of sweat on his forehead trickled down the side of his face and he shuffled uncomfortably. 'How could Neerdorf be alive!'

Chapter 12

Apart from meeting the medical team, the hospital visit had not been very fruitful. Erik and his mother had learned that Gert was in a bad way and had a 50/50 chance of recovery. He was unrecognisable in his hospital bed, wrapped in bandages and sheets, hooked up to a myriad of machines and tubes with monitors bleeping and doctors dashing in and out of his private room. The police had a guard on the door, not that he instilled much by way of confidence as he was more interested in the senior nurse than he was with anyone else who might be entering the room.

Arriving at the villa, Erik and Mrs Neerdorf found it locked up and empty, Thomas was no-where to be seen. Erik walked around to the back, and all was still and quiet. 'I'll ring him mum, he's probably just nipped out' stabbing the mobile number for Thomas into his phone he had a feeling something was terribly wrong. Thomas knew they were due to arrive, and he just wouldn't leave them, effectively locked out…what is going on…the phone started to ring.

'Erik, I can explain…'
'What the hell is going on Thomas, me and mum are stuck outside the house, no-one is here, we're tired, thirsty. If anyone sees us, stood here with our bags and cases, we'll look like we've been evicted or something ' Erik dramatised the situation but was clearly angry and his tired frustration was evident.
Thomas took a breath and listened for a few seconds at his brother's tirade 'I'm at the police station, I've been arrested and detained…'
'you've been what?' Erik was stunned into silence. What has his brother got himself into, what else could go wrong? 'This better be good Thomas'.
'I need you to come and pay the bail so I can get out of here'.
'What the fuck….? Thomas, what have you done?'
'Nothing Erik, I'll explain when you get me out, but hurry please'.
'I'm not moving an inch until I know what is going on here Thomas. Plus…' he paused and looked around to make sure the driver and his mother were out of earshot 'I can't bring mum to the police station, she has enough to cope with without this'.
'Just sort it out Erik, for once, just think about it, produce a solution and get me out of this cell'.
'Shit, shit, shit' Erik spat the words into the phone.
'They're taking my phone back off me Erik, I need to go…'
The phone went dead, and Erik just stood in the courtyard, alone, feeling helpless, wondering what had just happened.

Chapter 13

Targ arrived at his office early, not having slept much that night, taking the dozing duty manager by surprise as he slammed the door shut. With an alarming start the officer sprang into action 'err, good morning, sir…'

'Never mind all that, as soon as Demetriou arrives, send him immediately to my office' Targ didn't wait for a response and stormed off to find his desk, stopping at the machine on his way to get a hot, strong coffee. Sat behind his desk, he mulled over the conversation he'd had with the Commander and just couldn't shake the sense of foreboding the brief mention of Gregor Illianov had created. Who was this guy and why was he on this island? More importantly, why did he not know about it? Targ was unusually worried. Normally, the world was an easy place for him to exist in, he ran his affairs carefully but had learned to do it without much effort. Other people suffered stress not him, but, now at this very moment he too was tense, his stomach knotted, he struggled to think clearly. The rap on the glass in the door brought him round though. Targ looked up and shouted 'come' to the apparition that stood behind the frosted glass, knowing who it was. The door opened swiftly, and Alexis entered. He too, looked drained and like he'd not slept much, and he hadn't shaved either which was out of character for this normally pristine officer. 'Ah, Demetriou' Targ chose to adopt a formal approach 'come in and take a seat'. Not allowing for any pleasantries the Chief of Police got straight down to business 'what do you know of Gregor Illianov?'

The question was direct and took Alexis by surprise. He was expecting to be grilled about the report and his questioning of the difficult, evasive hotel manager. 'Gregor Illianov?' Alexis questioned and then added curiously 'he is a maintenance man at the hotel, he showed me the key cupboard in the staff room and provided a statement about the security of the keys.' He took a pause waiting for Targ to reveal why he had an interest in this inconspicuous little man, but it didn't come.

'Carry on' Targ instructed, eyes fixed on the young officer.

'Well, that's about it really, sir'. Alexis began to feel even more uncomfortable as he felt the stare bore into his face 'I took his statement and then he left, to go home I presume'.

'Right, this is important Alexis. The name of Gregor Illianov must not appear in any reporting relating to this or any other matter. That man does not exist as far as we are concerned, and it must remain that way. Do you understand?'

Alexis felt the heat rising in his neck 'not really sir, like I said, he made a statement and so…'

Targ cut him off mid-sentence 'no he didn't'.

'Sorry, what?'

'That man didn't provide a statement to you. You must be mistaken, and I'd suggest that if your report has somehow included a mention of that name, you need to… correct it' Targ thought carefully about his words.

'I, erm, I don't understand, sorry sir. I did get a statement from Gregor…'

'STOP! Listen carefully Alexis. Forget that name, remove it from your memory and any reporting that you might have, inadvertently, included in your summary.'

'You want me to amend evidence sir?'

'Alexis, consider this a lesson in life and a good way to move your career along faster that it looks like it might right now. I, your senior officer, am telling you that you must have made a mistake if you think that you met and took a statement from a man with this name. It is crucial that you realise that mistake and take action to correct it. Am I clear?'

Alexis was sweating, his face flushed with anxious nervousness, he felt his shoulders tighten and he clasped his hands tightly so that his knuckles showed white.

'AM I CLEAR' Targ shouted

'I think so sir, but…'

'Good' Targ interrupted 'let me see your report in the next half hour and we can then draw a line under this and move on'.

Alexis gulped audibly 'But what about the rest of the investigation, there are things that need to be, err, understood better'.

'No Alexis, the investigation is over. Nothing happened apart from a drunken tourist fell over a balcony. At worst, the Health and Safety Department will issue a fine and instruct the hotel to make the balconies safer. That isn't our concern, and we have a police station to run'.

Alexis sat, missing the cue to leave, fixed to his seat. 'I have to say sir, that I am not comfortable with the way this is ending'.

Targ looked at the squirming youngster across the desk 'well, manage it Alexis, you have half an hour to get your final draft report onto my desk, and I don't want it by e-mail just yet, I want to read it first. Thank you, Alexis'. Targ showed Alexis his hand and the way to the door.

Closing the door behind him, Alexis wondered about the exchange he had just been a part of and rued the day he thought about joining the Police force to make a positive difference to society. Despondent at the thought of falsifying evidential documents and mystified as to what and who Gregor Illianov was, Alexis sat at his desk in the communal office and thought about what he was going to do in the next half hour.

Morgan had organised a self-drive car for Erik and taken Mrs Neerdorf to the 5-star Diamond Bay Hotel just outside the centre of Kos for lunch and a drink and arranged to meet back at the villa later that afternoon. Erik arrived at the police station and entered the lobby, striding over to the reception desk where the duty officer sat, alert but looking weary and untidy. Erik studied him as he crossed the floor and decided that this is how it was in Greece; it must be something to do with the heat. 'Hello' he addressed the officer 'I am Erik Neerdorf, I'm here to get my brother Thomas'.

The policeman looked uninterested but responded 'you've come to pay the bail?'

Erik dismissed the question 'can I see him please and his lawyer too'.

'There is no lawyer, just the prisoner'.

Erik shook at the thought of his brother being called a prisoner.

'Follow me' instructed the officer as he led Erik through the open plan office, past the two on duty policemen, sat at their desks doing their bit to uphold the law on this little island. At the back of the room, they pass through a heavy wooden door into a darkened corridor that had 6 doors off it, each one an individual cell designed to securely hold drunks, petty thieves, and wayward tourists. The lock to number 2 opened easily with the oversized iron key attached the oversized chain hooked onto the policeman's belt. 'There you go' he said gesturing to Erik to enter.

'Erik, thank god, are you alone?' Thomas looked weary, drawn, and pale as he stood to welcome his twin brother.

Erik audibly gasped at the sight greeting him and immediately felt a greater sense of dread 'Thomas, what's going on?'

Before he had the chance to answer the policeman intervened 'you stay here with your brother whilst I get the paperwork completed, I can then take your payment and you can be on your way'.

Erik and Thomas sat on the flat, uncomfortable bench that ran across the wall underneath the barred window. It was open to allow the air to flow but it was still immensely hot and humid from the high afternoon sun.

'Thomas, you look awful. What the hell is going on?' Erik's voice was strained, and his face etched with emotion as he sat alongside his stable, sensible, usually bright sibling.

' Something bad is happening Erik...'

'Yes, I sort of realised that when dad had his incident' Erik chose incident instead of accident on purpose.

'No, it's more than that, I can't figure it out though'. He paused for a few seconds, ' Erik, the money has disappeared' he let the words hang whilst Erik digested the enormity of what he was saying.

'What money?' Erik's face stretched further, and his eyes widened.

'The payment dad collected from Rome, the $5 million that was paid into the bank by dad. The bank are saying it never happened, that he never visited the bank and they've no account of the money...at all.'

'But...but dad told us he had deposited the money; he has a deposit reference, and the balance showed the account was five million positive. I don't understand Thomas, who is telling you this?'

'The Director of Cullis Vaults, he told me that they have no record of the deposit reference, that it doesn't register on their systems and that our account with them has been dormant for the last year. I pressed him of course I did, but it sort of got out of hand and he called the police, which is why I have spent the last few hours in here and I missed your arrival at the house. I'm sorry Erik...'

'Stop, just stop. What are you saying?'

'Yes, it's hard to fathom isn't it' the brothers sat in silence for a few minutes.

Erik spoke again first, 'What about the two priest's dad met with? They should be able to validate that he at least had the money and what about the police? What are they doing to find this missing money?'

'They aren't interested Erik. The bank told them what they told me, so to them, the church, they have paid us what is owed and anything that happened after that is none of their concern. The police now simply want to process my arrest and get me out of their hair'.

The duty policeman walked back to the front desk and opened a drawer, taking out the charge sheet and a release form. Alexis followed him 'who is that in the cells?' he enquired.

'Just a crazy Dutchman claiming the bank has lost a few million dollars. He got a bit loud and threatening so he's just cooling off for a while. I've not decided if he'll appear in court yet, I might just let him go with a caution'.

'what's his name?' Alexis strained to look at the charge sheet 'is it Neerdorf?'

'How would you know that?' the duty officer retorted with surprise.

'Can I see him?'

'What about?'

'Something that happened yesterday at one of the hotels in town'.

'I don't see why not but be quick as the boss wants the guy out as quickly as possible and without any fuss, he said'.

Alexis thought for a second, he definitely didn't want to upset Targ even more than he apparently had already done so. 'I'll just pop my head in if that's ok, I'll be very quick'.

Alexis moved quickly across the office and into the corridor. Seeing the door open and the two brothers sat inside he entered tentatively 'Mr Neerdorf, hello I'm Officer Demetriou can I ask you some questions about your father please' he looked directly at Thomas, but it was Erik who responded.

'No'. He spat the words out. 'We want to ask you some questions about what happened to our father and where the fuck is the money he was looking after'.

The response took Alexis off guard as he realised that he shouldn't be here in this cell with these two people, if his boss found out, he'd be enraged. 'Look, I'm trying to help, I'm the investigating officer looking into what took place at the hotel.' He spoke quickly. 'Where are you staying, it'll be safer for each of us if we have this conversation away from here'.

The corridor door opened, and the duty guard appeared 'time's up Alexis, and the boss is looking for you'.

Before any more could be said, Alexis turned and stepped out of the cell, stopping for a brief moment he looked over his shoulder, 'I'll catch-up with you Mr Neerdorf wait for me to call you.'

He then continued to his desk where he picked up a copy of his final, redacted report and went off to find Targ.

The shouts could be heard by everyone in the station. 'WHAT DO YOU NOT UNDERSTAND DEMETRIOU?' Targ's violent verbal outburst was totally unexpected and shook Alexis to the core.

'But you told me to remove the guy's name sir, and that's what I have done. Convention states that…'

'FUCK YOUR CONVENTION'. Targ sat for a second, clearly fuming that this junior officer was trying his patience and playing corporate games. 'a redaction might as well be the same thing as leaving his name in' the voice steadied as Targ tried to remain calm 'pick a name and put it in place of those redaction marks. Any name you choose is fine by me as long as it isn't Illianov. Don't ask any more questions, don't even think about it, just do as I say'. Targ sat back and eyed his quarry, stony faced, unapologetic, frightening.

'I, err, want to be clear sir, you want me to falsify…'

'Get out Demetriou' his voice was quiet and menacing 'get out of my office. The next time I see you I want that completed' he jabbed his finger at the paper report sat on his desk. 'and completed to my satisfaction. Is that clear enough?' he growled, and saliva foamed at the corners of his mouth.

Alexis picked up the report and silently, quickly exited the office. He sat at his computer and did what he had been asked to do without thinking any more about the implications. He looked back through his arrest files and chose one at random, inserting the name of a male who was caught drink driving last month and had returned to Sweden last week. Feeling numb and confused, he dropped the report into an internal envelope and left if outside Targ's office to be picked up when his boss next passed. Alexis then left the building and drove to the café where he spent the next hour contemplating his future. A text message pinged, and he glanced to see it was from Targ 'report is fine, e-mail it to me this afternoon. Case Closed'

Alexis did what was asked but he knew the case was anything but closed, especially as he was going to see the Neerdorf brothers after breakfast tomorrow.

Chapter 14

Hindle was deeply troubled by what he had learned. He had tried and failed to establish contact with the Germans to get a definitive understanding of what had taken place at the hotel. The fact that Gert and Anita were incommunicado wasn't in itself an issue, it was usual in the weeks after a mission but there was an emergency channel that remained always open, in both directions. The encrypted email server hosted deep inside the deep web was a safe and secure environment to maintain contact with some of Paul's least savoury connections. This was however also drawing a blank, which was out of character for these two collaborators and more importantly, outside of the contractual arrangement that existed between them. This situation was exacerbated by the fact that he had yet to speak with De Cathay who was under the impression that this episode with Neerdorf Securities was closed and that a new, more favourable, payment structure was to be discussed and agreed with Dirk Neardorff's successor. Sometimes, he wondered how he got himself into such predicaments, he was after all, a man of God and all that stood for.

He contemplated his position as he walked out, through the wooded grounds that lay at the rear of the Basilica that housed his office. It was dry and cool, very crisp underfoot and the trees were alive with birdsong as the little creatures raced around, to feed themselves and their new families. Paul stood and watched in wonderment for a few seconds. This was God's work at its best, nature in all its fantastic glory. Life was all about, living out the word of His Lord in spectacular fashion, existing, growing, nurturing, creating life and ensuring that the ongoing everlasting circle continued unabated. Paul pulled his cassock tight over his shoulders and repositioned his zucchetto, so it felt more secure. He breathed in the cool air around him and continued his meandering stroll along the dirt track pathway. 'Paul, I've been looking for you' De Cathays voice startled and immediately increased Hindle's anxiety. 'What are you doing out here, all on your own? Are you alright?'
'Hello Georges, I'm just getting some fresh air and doing a bit of thinking'.
'Well, now that I've got you, let's walk together and you can tell me what you have organised for Friday'.
Friday afternoon was when Georges let his guard down a little in Paul's opinion, as he indulged one of his more unorthodox Christian past-times. Relieved that De Cathays focus was not connected to Neerdorf Securities, Paul smiled. 'Yes, you're in for a treat Georges. I have a new girl flying in from Amsterdam. She comes very highly recommended by my supplier, very discreet, young, dark skinned, petite, just what you asked for. '
De Cathay sneered and Paul shivered at the grotesque picture that stood next to him.
'Excellent, as always Paul. Thank you very much. Now, what's this I am hearing about the Kos incident' His face changed to stone and Paul could feel the intensity of De Cathays stare boring into him.
'What have you heard?' Paul countered, hoping that Georges wasn't fully up to speed.
'I'm sure it isn't true Paul, but I've been advised that the CEO of Neerdorf Securities is seriously hurt and lying in a hospital bed on the island of Kos'. De Cathays tone was questioning but threatening at the same time. Paul thought carefully for a few seconds, if he positioned this wrong then he would be in a very precarious situation. 'I am trying to establish an accurate position Georges, I'll be clearer by this evening but at the moment, I'm

taking the view as we understood it to be yesterday. Once that is clarified though, I'll let you know.'

There was a silence as the two men continued to walk through the trees. Paul felt deeply unnerved but said nothing further, he definitely wasn't going to compromise his position by adding anything further. Georges thought deeply for a while. 'People are talking Paul and my experience tells me that what they are saying has substance. Don't take your time with this, we…' he emphasised the word, 'need a quick resolution to the gossip my friend'. His voice softened and Paul felt a hand on his shoulder that was meant to be comforting but had the opposite effect.

'Georges' Paul's voice was tense 'I had Eduardo Musso on the phone earlier asking a similar question. He is showing a close interest…'

'More reason to shut it down quickly then. I can handle him don't worry about that, but I need to be sure that nothing can bite either of us' again he made it clear that they were handling this, whatever it was, together. 'Get back to me later today Paul and we can put it all to bed'.

'Musso also said that he had recruited a replacement for Alberto?'

'Really?' De Cathay appeared surprised and a bit rattled 'I'll look into that too, thanks for the tip off'. De Cathays mobile phone rang, and he glanced down at the display. 'I need to get this, we'll catch-up this evening Paul', and off he went, back in the direction that they had met.

Paul continued to walk and found the exit gate that led out onto a stone pathway and onwards to the piazza. The immediate and contrasting bustle of the ever-growing tourist trade that amassed in this relatively small area made him frown a little, and he put his head down as he strode out amongst the mixed crowds of worshipers and sightseers. Some acknowledged his rank, nodded, crossed themselves and/or smiled, others just got out of his way as his purposeful demeanour carried him across the old stone flags in the direction of the ancient Basilica that was his intended destination. 'Senor Hindle' he heard a distant muffled call but wasn't sure it was actually his name that was being shouted across the square. 'Cardinal Hindle, wait, please' it was clearer and closer, but he kept walking with his head down, determined to get to the side gate he could see in the distance. A hand clasped onto his shoulder, and he had to stop and turn 'oh thank you, Cardinal just a moment of your time'. Paul stared into a vaguely familiar face and then jumped in startled horror as the TV camera appeared through the slowly gathering crowd and pointed its intrusive lens towards the cornered Priest. 'What? Who are you please, how do you know my name?' Paul tried to remain calm, remembering his training, knowing that he wasn't about to give an interview to anyone let alone Sky News. 'Hello, hello, I'm Jessica Haig from the Sky News team and it's my job to know who you are.' She smiled a most insincere smile and continued. 'We're here reporting on this week's general audience and wondered if you can give us a few words about how you think it will go?' The camera zoomed in on a close-up of Paul's face and waited for a response. Paul fought his instinct to tell the journalist to leave him alone but media intrusion, as he had been taught many times, came with the territory. Calmly, professionally, he looked the journalist directly in the face 'I'm deeply sorry Ms Haig, I am not in a position to comment. You should call our media relations team, I'm sure you have their contact details'. The journalist, clearly expecting the rehearsed response quickly came back 'do you know the content of this week's address?'

'I'm terribly sorry my dear, I'm not privy to the content of the address…'

'Is it related to the recent bad press the church has had?' she pressed on, unfazed by the priest's decline to comment.

Paul pushed on through the crowd and passed the cameraman 'get out of my way' he hissed out of earshot of the microphone. He wondered what bad press she was talking about though but wasn't going to ask her to clarify.

'Senor Hindle, can you tell us what you know about the recent attempted murder of a senior Dutch financier in Greece or the death of a foreign agent in Malta last year?'

Startled, Paul's heart skipped a beat, and he became desperate to get out of the glare of the camera that had turned to watch him scurry away. As he reached his destination, he glanced back to see the journalist doing a piece to camera, gesticulating in his general direction. Now he felt even more anxiety, and as he entered the building, panting from the pressure of his encounter and subsequent escape from the news hacks, he felt his legs weaken and beads of sweat break across his forehead. He found a seat in the corridor and quickly sat down, shoulders slumped, head in hands, thoughts slamming into his brain. What the hell is going on? How has Sky News got onto these things? How do they know who he is? What does he do next?

Chapter 15

Katharine Neerdorf had lived a charmed life. Even before her marriage to the suave, ambitious money man, her life was one of privilege as she was born into a family of wealth and high political influence. Her father was a self-made millionaire, and her mother came from a long line of titled gentry. She hadn't really wanted for anything at any time in her forty odd years but now, as she stood in the conservatory of this rented villa, looking out over the pristine gardens, feeling the heat of the mid-morning sun, holding a steaming cup of hot black coffee, she felt lost. Her husband was on the edge of death, she had no idea why, she didn't know anything about the business that had occupied him and their two sons' for as long as she could remember, she didn't even know if her sons knew how to carry on the business should the worse happen. Katharine had never had to deal with this sort of stress at any time in her past and she didn't like it.

'Mother, I've asked Morgan to take you to the hospital so you can get an update on dad, and then if you like, he'll take you into the centre. The market is on today, it might be good for you to do some shopping' Thomas hoped she would go, as he didn't want her around when the policeman arrived.

'Thomas, I've never shopped in a market in my life' she turned and faced him, knowing he was trying to get rid if her for a while 'If you want me out of the way just say so, I'm not stupid and don't take pity on me'.

'No mum, I'm not trying to get rid of you. I just think…'

'Save it Thomas, I'm going out anyway. I have a friend on the island who I've arranged to visit, so your problem is solved'.

Thomas looked on and said nothing. He could see that his mother was distressed and hadn't slept well. 'Ok, take care and have a nice time. If you need anything, Morgan has instructions to do whatever is needed.'

Katharine looked back at him 'what does that mean? 'whatever is needed?' You make him sound like some sort of hit man'.

Thomas looked weary, he could do without his mother's contrariness 'I mean, if you want to go on somewhere, he is at your disposal for the day'.

'Thank you' she responded dismissively and walked back through the kitchen and into the large lounge.

Thomas opened the conservatory door and stepped into the gardens, taking a seat at the solid wood table and bench, he closed his eyes and enjoyed the feeling of the warm sun that was just hovering above the line of trees at the bottom of the expansive lawn.

'Hey brother, I've brought you a drink' Erik appeared holding two full glasses of freshly squeezed, chilled orange juice.

'Thanks Erik, I was just taking in some rays for a few minutes.'

'a few minutes?' Erik laughed 'I've been watching you this last half hour! Morgan has taken mum to the hospital to see dad and then she's visiting some old friend later'.

'Half an hour, wow I must have dozed off.' Thomas felt better for it but hadn't realised how long he'd been sat there 'thanks for the drink, it's just what I need,' skipping over his mother's plans he looked casually at his phone, checking for messages or calls. 'The policeman will be here shortly, how are we going to play this Erik?'

'we'll let him tell us what he knows, and what is happening with the investigation. Our part is to forge a partnership with the cops and let them know we trust them and can work with them to find who did this to dad and who has our money'.

Thomas listened and recognised the clarity of thought around the pre meeting plan that his brother demonstrated time and again in his relationship director role. There was really no-one better at fostering business affiliations to drive the absolute best commercial returns.

They heard the crunch of tyres on gravel as Alexis arrived in his battered old Clio. It had seen better days, but it continued to serve him well and it didn't matter much anyway, as the island was so small, he wasn't in danger of running up the miles much higher any time soon.

Thomas greeted him with a friendly smile and warm handshake 'thanks for coming Mr Demetriou'.

'Alexis please. Only the boss calls me by my family name, and then only when he's mad at me' the policeman chuckled and followed Thomas through to the garden where Erik was sat and had already poured the chilled sparkling water, adorned with a slice of lemon. The three men sat and exchanged pleasantries for a short while before Alexis offered his sympathies regarding Mr Neerdorf senior and that was the cue Thomas had been waiting for. 'Thanks Alexis, yes he's in a bad way but comfortable. Mum is with him this morning, so we'll have a progress update later I'd imagine. Maybe at this juncture you could bring us to speed with your work on the matter'. The brothers both looked intently at Alexis and offered a further smile. They had agreed that it was important to keep the conversation flowing and make sure that their guest remained relaxed.

'Well, the current position hasn't moved much I'm afraid' Alexis lied. 'I've spent a couple of days at the hotel, interviewing the staff and reviewing the CCTV footage but we haven't yet got any evidence of wrongdoing or indeed a clear idea of what took place. I was really hoping that you guys might be able to fill some gaps in our knowledge to assist us to keep moving forward'. He maintained a friendly eye contact with both of his hosts and worked hard to keep his voice level and of a clear and dominant tone.

'What do you need from us?' Erik came back quickly 'we weren't even on the island when this happened'.

'Well, could you clarify the reason that Mr Neerdorf was in Kos? Our search has so far shown that he left Amsterdam and arrived in Rome before hopping down here, all over a few days.'

Thomas intervened with a slight show of his hand to Erik 'he had a business meeting in Rome then he was going to spend a few days here on Kos, relaxing. Mum was going to join him, and they planned to return home after the weekend.'

'Who was the meeting with?'

Erik this time took the lead. 'We can't tell you that, the nature of our business dictates a certain level of confidentiality that if broken might place the client in a difficult position'. Alexis smiled and took a sip of his drink, 'yes I get that, but as I understand them, confidentiality agreements don't extend to criminal investigations Erik'.

Thomas thought for a second, 'Erik we have trust the agencies we need to work with if we are to get to the bottom of this matter.' He turned to address Alexis, but then had second thoughts 'Erik is right. Our client in Rome would not wish us to disclose their identity but we can tell you that they are very high profile, in a global sense, and bringing them into this matter could cause huge reputational damage.'

Alexis quickly accepted their position and went with it to see what else might come out in the exchange 'ok, so this meeting, did it go well, was everything achieved that your father set out to achieve?'

'Yes, absolutely. It was very productive, and we were satisfied with the outcomes'. Thomas thought it best that the church wasn't disrespected or implicated at this stage.

'And did either of you speak with your father between the end of the meeting and his tragic accident?'

'I did' replied Thomas 'and we don't accept that it was accident'.

Alexis sensed some aggression for the first time during their meeting 'no, of course not. Apologies. It's difficult for us all to imagine what happened but I must remind you that we have no evidence yet of any wrongdoing or any threat surrounding your father...'

'No evidence?' Erik jumped in, his voice slightly raised but not yet shouting, his face however was betraying his growing anger as it started to burn red 'my father was pushed out of that window by someone who wanted him out of the way'.

Alexis remained calm despite his surprise at the outburst 'how would you know that Erik and more importantly, why would someone want to do that?'

'it's all very co-incidental don't you think' Erik's tone had turned sarcastic.

'co-incidental?' Alexis questioned. A feeling of foreboding starting to creep over him, what else didn't he know about this investigation.

Thomas put his hand up 'Erik, wait a moment' He looked directly into Demetriou's eyes 'I'm not sure we are speaking with the right level of authority here Alexis. Just what part of this matter are you investigating?'

Alexis felt uncomfortable, he was acting outside of his orders here, if this got out of hand and Targ found out he'd be for the high jump. 'Mr Neerdorf, please, I am the investigating officer and I have a full view of the whole case. I have reported my findings thus far...'

'But you have no findings, you've told us that twice now' Erik was getting more frustrated with the lack of clarity or apparent understanding.

'What co-incidences are you referring to please' Alexis regained some composure and enquired further. There was something else going on here , something that he was as yet unaware of, but he felt, was a critical part of the case.

Thomas realised that the police hadn't connected his visit to the bank with what had happened to his father, and he wasn't sure if divulging the fact that $5m was missing would be helpful at this time. Erik didn't allow much more thinking time however 'my father deposited a significant sum of money at Cullis Vaults and that seems to have disappeared. Add to that, a mysterious and unfortunate *incident'* he spat out the word 'that may have killed my father, and I think you might conclude that there is a glaring and obvious co-incidence in the events that have taken place on your island.'

Stunned and realising that the arresting officer hadn't thoroughly interviewed Thomas to even understand why he was at the bank or completed the sign off report properly Alexis thought quickly...it's not *my* island! And responded shakily 'what is a significant sum of money?'

'Try five...million...dollars. Do you understand our frustration now Alexis?'

Before he had the time to take it in or respond his phone rang. Looking at the display he saw with anguish that it was Targ, could this situation get any more awkward 'sorry guys, I need to take this' Alexis stood and walked towards the bottom of the lawn and out of ear shot.

'yes, boss' he tried hard to sound relaxed and steady.

'Alexis, where are you, I was expecting you in the office by now?'

'I just stopped off, there was an incident with a stolen car last night and I thought…'

'Ok, ok, get yourself on the move quickly. We have a report of a body over by the jetty near the harbour at Mastichari, get over there and let me know what's going on.'

The phone went dead, and Alexis stood, rooted to the spot. He took a deep breath and turned 'I'm sorry something has happened, and I'm needed back at the station.'

'What?' Erik sprang out of his seat 'we're only just starting here. What sort of police force is this?'

'Clearly a small one Erik. Let Alexis get on with he has to do, and we can catch-up later' Thomas, ever the diplomat, tried to smooth the way.

'Yes, Thomas let me call you later this afternoon with an update.'

When they had shown him out Thomas closed the door and looked long and hard at Erik. 'Do you think they have any idea about what they are doing at all?'

'we'll find out later today wont we.'

Thomas' phone rang 'it's mum' he said alarmed 'hi mum is everything ok?'

'No Thomas, please come to the hospital, bring Erik.' Her voice quivered with emotion.

'Mum? What's the matter? Is dad, ok?' he could hear the pain as she spoke.

'The surgeon is arranging for the local priest to come and give the last rites' her sobs were loud and the words broken as she tried to speak 'he maybe has a few hours Thomas, I don't know what to do.'

She cried into the phone and Thomas looked across at his brother, ashen faced and starting to shake 'we're on our way mum, just stay where you are.' The phone went dead. 'Get the keys to the hire car Erik, its dad I'll explain on the way.'

Chapter 16

Alexis pulled off the central main road that runs south to north through the middle of the island, at Antimachia and took the minor road, glancing regularly at the amazing views until he arrived at the harbour in the little old fishing village of Mastichari. He immediately saw the ambulance and a small gathering at the water's edge. As he pulled over and got out of the car, he was approached by one of the ambulance crew. 'What have we got?' Alexis asked. 'It's a strange one to be sure' the female medic responded. Alexis noted that she looked shaken 'we've got a murder I reckon. It's a male, looks mid to late 50's, with a single gunshot to the back of the head. His hands are tied too'.

Alexis walked with the medic over to the body, choosing to walk around the small crowd of around a dozen onlookers rather than through them. 'Right, first things first. Let's get a screen around this area please so we can work, I'll organise a SOCO and get rid of these people.' He took his phone from his pocket and rang the boss, who answered almost straight away.

'Demetriou, how are you getting on?'

'We have a murder sir, so I'll need a SOCO quite quickly and before the tide turns' Alexis moved closer to the body as he spoke and noticed the familiar shirt with the Hotel Logo on the shoulder and chest.

'Do we have any ID yet?' Targ asked.

'Not yet sir but...' Alexis stopped short, stunned into silence as he recognised the face of the dead man. The head had a big shocking hole blown out of the forehead by the bullet travelling through from its entry point at the back. The face was grey, rugged, and heavily blood stained but there was no doubt at all that the man laying dead on the pebble beach, tied to the harbour poles was Gregor Illianov.

'Alexis? What's happening?' Targ's voice was strained and high pitched.

'Sir, I think it's Illianov....'.

Both men went silent, taking in the information and both feeling a sense of dread, for slightly different reasons. Targ imagining the ramifications from Athens when HQ found out that the police protection programme had been breached in the most serious way. Alexis, formulating a connection between his investigation, the missing money he'd learned about earlier and this brutal assassination of one of his witnesses.

Targ was first to speak, 'as soon as the SOCO get there Demetriou, I want you back here. Come straight to my office and do not divulge that man's name to anyone. As far as we are concerned, he has not yet been identified.'

The phone went dead before Alexis could respond, not that he felt able. He held onto a nearby post as he felt his knees wobble and the bile rose quickly in his throat and forced him to double over as the contents of his stomach splashed onto the pebbles under his feet. He felt one of the medics grab his arm and lead him to the sea wall 'come on, sit down here. It's a gruesome sight'.

Alexis did as he was told and thanked the carer. Smiling through his thin lips, he nodded his appreciation and rested, head in hands for a few seconds. He heard a car draw up and two doors open. Glancing across, he recognised the two officers who got out and started to don their protective whites and boots. 'What can you tell us Alexis?'. The tallest of the two men walked over to the wall 'oh dear, is it that bad my friend?' he laughed 'I always had you down as one of the stronger ones Demetriou'.

Alexis ignored the comments and relayed the little information that he had about the scene in front of them and then made his excuses and returned to his own car. Driving the short 12 km's back to the station, Alexis tried to steady his nerves and think about his meeting with the dead man, and what Targ might have waiting for him.

Hindle knocked on De Cathays office door and waited. 'Enter' Georges' voice was always loud and carried an air of authority that to some was always intimidating. Paul entered and saw his friend on the old desk phone that sat on the edge of his 300-year-old solid oak desk. Georges gestured for him to sit down in one of the two equally antique, ornate chairs that were placed across from his own, majestic seat. 'Eduardo, I need to leave it there, my next meeting has arrived' Georges smiled across at Paul 'I'll come and see you tomorrow morning and we'll discuss it in detail, but please, don't worry, there is no substance to this at all.' He returned the handset to its cradle and turned to face Paul 'that's Musso, he thinks he is close to uncovering a conspiracy'.
'And is he?' Paul retorted quickly.
'I was hoping you might be able to help me with that Paul. We saw your TV appearance the other day' he smirked 'I thought you handled the snoop well. So does everyone, well done'.
Hindle squirmed as he recalled the encounter 'I don't know where they get their information from, but she appeared to know more than is comfortable'.
'Let them think what they want Paul, they have no evidence and so it's just gossip as far as we are concerned. Don't let it bother you, we have more control over the hacks than you might realise'.
Paul relaxed a little, but not too much, his reason for visiting was not a good one. 'I have information about Neerdorf…'
'Ah yes, not long for this world as I understand it'.
Paul looked startled 'what do you mean Georges?'
'Tell me what you have found out first Paul.'
De Cathay was clearly playing with him, and he didn't like it. 'Neerdorf survived his fall and is in intensive care. Its currently 50/50 whether he survives but I have a connection in the area who can help us.'
'I'm not sure that will be necessary. My sources tell me that he has a few hours at most. He has had the last rites delivered and his family are gathered…waiting' De Cathay looked deep into Paul's eyes and smiled a sneering grin 'you see Paul, I too have connections, people on the ground so to speak.'
Paul chose not to ask any further about these sources knowing that sometimes, the less he knew the better.
De Cathay stood and walked around his desk towards the window 'I sensed in our last conversation Paul, that we might be losing a bit of control, so I took some decisive action'.
'I'm not sure that is fair Georges' Paul had started to sweat a little 'I have a strong and clear view of where things are.'
De Cathay turned swiftly, making Paul jump a little 'fair Paul? Nothing is fair; however, I need to make sure that our backs are protected too, especially when people like Musso are sniffing around, and information is being leaked to the press.'
'So, the fact that Neerdorf is…nearing the end?' Paul left the sentence unfinished.
'Let's just say that one of the Churches supporters, offered to help Mr Neerdorf to reach his final destination and relieve his pain and suffering. It is without doubt a mercy mission Paul.'

De Cathay smiled a most holy smile and returned to his seat. 'Needless to say, Paul, we'll be extending our sympathies to the family and then we'll invite them here to review our arrangement. We need to test them and establish just how accurate their knowledge around our arrangement is and how detailed their record keeping is. When I get any news from Greece, I'll let you know, although, I'm sure you are aware, really, it is you who should keep me informed of such matters.'

Paul was stung by the insinuation that he had failed to keep abreast of the situation and further disturbed that De Cathay had connections operating across his own remit. He stood and thanked Georges for the update. As he opened the door De Cathay glanced over 'one more thing Paul, I trust I can rely on you to stay on top of the other matters we have discussed'.

'Everything remains in order Georges' Paul was irked by the remarks but stayed calm, closing the door quietly behind him, he tensed his fists and grimaced as he walked away to his own office, deeply bothered that De Cathay had an operative, live in an area that Paul assumed to control. He needed to find out who that was before he was undermined any further.

Chapter 17

The brothers arrived at the hospital and made quickly to their father's room. As they arrived, a priest was comforting their mother, holding her in his arms so his cassock wrapped around her shoulders, the sons could hear her sobbing. Medical staff were watching the screens and administering drugs by needle and topping up the intravenous drips. 'Mother' Thomas spoke softly 'what is the news?'

One of the doctors turned and introduced himself in a strong English accent 'ah, you must be Thomas' he held out his hand and 'Erik. I'm sorry to meet you in these circumstances. Your father has had an unexpected reaction, we think to one of the stabilising drugs he's been getting, so we've cleaned that out and are administering a different one now along with some antidote to counter the bad reaction'.

Thomas looked on bemused, he was trying to take in all this information, but he was struggling.

'What substance?' Erik was less calm.

'let's go to my office, follow me please. The doctor turned and walked out of the room without waiting for a response. The brothers followed, looking quizzically at each other. They arrived at a row of offices, all with white doors and a small window in each. This one was adorned with large silver lettering 'Dawson McKeown – Chief Medical Officer'.

Inside, they were invited to sit down 'can I get you both a drink?'

Dawson McKeown was a recent addition to the hospital staff having been recruited from St Bartholomew's in the City of London to take over the running of the private medical facility on the island. Having spent 20 Years in the hustle and bustle of the capital, he was getting to the stage of life where he wanted to experience something new whilst putting his extensive experience to good use. When approached, it took him less than a day to accept the position and after working out his 6 months' notice period moved his life and family, consisting of just his two cats, to a luxury villa overlooking the stunning Kochilari Bay. That was almost 12 months' ago to the day, and he hadn't once regretted making the move.

Dawson made two americano's from his office machine and placed them on the table 'sorry, I haven't introduced myself properly'. He sat opposite them and took a glass of water before stating his name and position as head of the hospital trust. 'Your father is in good hands' Dawson looked across the desk at the men sat opposite 'I think he is stabilising well and I'm confident that he will make a recovery and continue the recuperation process that we were overseeing before this incident'.

'So why the priest?' Erik was bemused and frustrated 'why does my mother think he's at death's door?'

Dawson considered his response carefully 'earlier today, your father had what looks like an allergic reaction to one of the drugs we have been giving him. It can happen, before you ask!' He anticipated the next question well 'occasionally, rarely, someone can react to a drug that has been administered over a period of time and that is what we think has happened here. We spotted it quickly and cleared out his system, then changed the range of drugs that he is now taking. During that time though, he was extremely ill, and we took the decision to call our priest to be on standby in case maters took a further turn for the worse. Thankfully, that hasn't happened.'

'And does mum know this?' Thomas asked gently.

'Yes, we broke the news that your father was reacting well, just before you arrived. Father Martins is looking after her at the moment, but you saw that'.

Relieved, the brothers relaxed a little. 'When will we be able to speak with him?' Thomas was keen to understand what his father could recall about the fall and more importantly what he did with the money.

'That I can't say just yet. We have him in an induced coma and need to manage that carefully so that he comes out of it in as good a condition as is possible. I must warn you though, there is a danger that he could be brain damaged, to what extent is impossible to say right now, but it is possible.'

Erik thought for a second 'thank you Doctor McKeown. It's important for us a family and for our business interests that our father comes out of this predicament as quickly as possible and compos mentis, so you must do whatever it takes, and we will make sure that you get whatever you need, so don't hesitate to ask us…for anything.'

'Thank you, Erik, we are well funded and have the best experience available in this part of Europe' Dawson smiled, 'but I will keep that in mind'.

There was a knock on the door and a nurse appeared 'Doctor, we have the patient stable, and he is now breathing comfortably'.

'Excellent news, thank you nurse' Dawson stood and smiled as the nurse made her exit. 'I think you can leave us to it now, he is reacting well to the treatment. If anything changes, I'll call you and of course feel free to visit any time you like.'

All three men stood and shook hands and Dawson showed them out, collecting Mrs Neerdorf on the way. As they drove away, Dawson turned to the physician and asked, 'do you have the toxicology report again please?' he took the file and returned to his office, closing the door behind him he sat and re-read the results of the tests the team had undertaken earlier. He scanned it, happy that everything seemed to be under control now and that they had indeed responded quickly when the patient had shown signs of poisoning. What bothered him was why there were traces of Fentanyl in the man's blood stream and how had it got there. His decision not to divulge that to the family was one that was designed to protect the hospital from claims of neglect or negligence, Dawson trusted his instincts but couldn't help but be worried that someone had tried to finish off this patient. He'd need to make sure that the staff were on high alert and upped their vigilance, he and the hospital couldn't afford to get embroiled in a scandal involving security and the potential murder of someone under their care.

Paul had made a few calls over the course of the past few days and called in some information from his more trusted contacts including his old friend Roger Barlow back in Amsterdam. It was him who had taken a call from De Cathay and identified a skilled, trustworthy operative based in Athens. Paul was taken aback that Barlow hadn't tipped him off but felt better in the fact that De Cathay didn't have a direct relationship with someone in the area. 'If it happens again Roger, please just let me know. He can be difficult to manage at the best of times without him running around thinking he is controlling things on my patch'.

'Sorry Paul, I just assumed that you would know, given how close you two seem to be.' Having confirmed the name and contact details of the operative, Paul made a secure call and introduced himself using the man's code name. 'How did the assignment go please?' he enquired.

'I managed to get past the security system and into his room relatively easily. The place was deserted at that time of the night, there was a guard on duty who was patrolling the grounds and the few staff who were on duty were all in the staff room. It was easy really. I administered the poison into his calf muscle and then left. It took less than five minutes from start to finish.'

'Good, well done. Payment will be in your account next time you care to look.' He ended the call and rang another number. 'Hello, can you tell me what the patient visiting times are, please'.

'Yes, for which patient?'

Paul hesitated, 'you're looking after my good friend Dirk Neerdorf'.

'I'm very sorry' the receptionist paused whilst looking at the patient roster. Paul held his breath waiting to hear the news.

'Mr Neerdorf isn't taking visits from anyone other than closest family, as his condition still hasn't improved enough'.

'Oh, so he's still in a coma then?' Paul pressed for further clarification.

'I'm not supposed to give out any information but yes, he's still in a coma'.

Paul put the phone down and thought for a moment. Neerdorf was a tough cookie for sure, what should he do now as the local police will be all over this attempted murder, and how will De Cathay react when he finds out? Hindle was relieved and worried at the same time. Relieved that Georges attempts to undermine him had failed but Neerdorf was still alive, that remained a huge threat to his position and that of the church.

Chapter 18

Alexis was shaking and sweating as he entered the station. The duty officer looked across at his 'Jesus, Alexis you look ill, what is the matter?'

'I'll be fine,' he lied 'is the boss in in his office?'

He walked towards the closed door before receiving an answer. He knocked on the door and waited to granted access. 'Come in' the growl was unmistakable and meant that Roman Targ was present and in a dangerously angry state of mind. 'Demetriou, what's taken you so long?' The senior officer gestured for Alexis to take a seat.

'Sorry sir, I had to wait for the SOCO guys to arrive'.

'Yes, and then go and clean yourself up I believe' Targ snorted 'weak stomach today?'

Alexis thought that the sarcasm was unnecessary and realised that he would be the butt of everyone's jokes over the coming weeks. He remained silent.

'Ok, so what the fuck do you know about this latest mess?'

Alexis drew breath, 'although it's not been formally confirmed the dead man is definitely Illianov and by the looks of it, he was executed. We have people at the scene right now and I'll get an update as soon as I can.'

'You need to know Demetriou, that this is the worst possible thing to happen on our patch in the history of the station, and you my friend are to blame'.

Alexis physically jolted in his seat 'but sir, how can you say that? I have maintained confidentiality regarding Illianov in everything I have done and produced'.

'What about that original report? Where is it?'

'It doesn't exist. I overwrote it when you told me to. There is only one copy of that report and I sent it only to you, by email, as instructed'.

'Well, someone close to you must have leaked it then, which ever way you look at it, the fact he is now dead follows your inter-action with him. That cannot be and is not a co-incidence. It's a mess and one we will need time to clear up. At least the case is closed now and no-one else will be sniffing around it'.

Alexis tensed 'well sir, I have some news on that'.

'Go on' Targ eyed Alexis with a deep dark stare, and the beginnings of a volcanic rage began as a tic behind his left eye.

'I saw the Neerdorf twins the other day, and they are alleging that their father was the subject of an attempted assassination'.

'What the…' he didn't finish the sentence but just sat staring at Alexis from across the desk. If he had been close enough, Alexis would have felt a punch to his jaw that would have probably sent him sprawling. Targ however, looked on open mouthed. 'I told you in no uncertain terms that THIS CASE IS CLOSED' the words rang out loud through the whole building. 'Are you stupid? Do you not understand what it means when a superior office gives you a command? Fuck me Demetriou, I'm lost for words' Targ sat back, literally unable to speak any further.

'Sir, they approached me, knowing that I was the investigating officer', he lied.

'Ex investigating officer' Targ corrected.

'They offered an explanation that was very plausible sir'.

Targ looked up, with a look of derision, 'there is no explanation Demetriou, the man fell from the balcony, and he was drunk'.

'But he had five million dollars with him sir, that has now disappeared. It seems someone has stolen the money and then tried to kill of Neerdorf'.

There was a silence.

'Bollocks'.

'Sir?' Alexis looked at his boss, exasperated and feeling desperate.

'That is bollocks. A drunken man falls out his hotel window and nearly dies, then his family, who own a struggling finance house appear, and claim there is a vast amount of money missing…and you take it all in and devise this story? I just hope their insurers aren't as gullible as you are. I'll say this one more time, stay away from this case, IT IS SHUT! DO YOU UNDERSTAND?'

Alexis took a deep breath 'what should I say to the family, they are expecting…'

'Expecting what?' Targ growled 'exactly what have you promised them?'

'nothing' Alexis lied again 'I just said I'd look at it to see if there might be a connection'.

Targ stood sharply, sending his chair spinning across the floor into the wall behind him.

'Your insubordination is without compare, I have never in all my life witnessed anything like it. You are finished Demetriou. I need to think about how I deal with you so go home, don't talk to anyone about this, I mean anyone, and wait for my call'.

'You're suspending me sir?' Alexis looked shocked, ashen faced and was starting to shake for the second time today.

'Not yet, I'm telling you to take the afternoon off. GO, GET OUT OF MY SIGHT…'

Alexis left without another word, made for his car and took the drive home, not really in a fit state to drive as his head was completely mixed up.

When he had left the office Targ, sat for a moment and took a long drink from his mug, the coffee was strong and still retained some heat. He picked up his desk phone and pressed the pre dial to Athens HQ. The Divisional Commander answered 'Roman, this is an unusual pleasure, what can I do for you?'

Targ established a mental image of his superior officer. She was a fearsome woman, very thick set with short dark hair and the coldest eyes he had ever encountered. He recounted the conversation that had just taken place in his office adding the news about the dead man. 'I think Demetriou has become a liability and is clearly out of control'.

'So, what do you want me to do Roman?' the Commander responded without offering an opinion.

'I want to transfer him out to another island maam, get him away from this mess he has caused and teach him a lesson'.

'And you think a quiet life on a smaller island will do that?'

The question surprised Targ 'well, yes, it's either that or we sack him but he's young and I can see some potential in him'.

'There is another way Roman.'

Targ sat up straight, what had he missed? He hated it when he got caught out like this 'go on maam'.

'Give him some more rope and see how he gets on. He'll either get himself into more trouble and make the decision for you, or he'll shine, and we'll thank him for it'.

'And what would be your suggestion around that?'

'I happen to know that Mr Neerdorf met with two senior members of the Vatican before his visit to Kos. I'd suggest that you send Demetriou over to Rome to see them and see what he can find out about that meeting and what they might know about subsequent events.'

Targ was bemused now 'what, who?' he stuttered momentarily 'are you saying that there is a chance that the Vatican might be involved in harming one of their business partners?'

'No. Not at all. I'm saying in the circumstances we should be seen to have an interest in this part of the investigation and see where Demetriou finds himself. I believe there are two Cardinals who saw Neerdorf, Hindle and De Cathay, I can open the doors to them if Demetriou needs any help.'

Targ though for a second 'OK I'll get him back in and get it organised.'

Before he had chance to put the phone down his boss added 'oh and one more thing. The bank on the island is out of bounds, make sure Demetriou stays away. Is that clear?'

'The bank, which bank? Why would we want to go making enquiries of the bank?'

'Cullis Vaults, the private place out near the airport. Just make sure it's off everyone's radar. And Roman, if I were you, I'd get up to speed with what the Neerdorf's are claiming has happened.' Targ cringed, feeling the rebuke from his superior and knowing that he should at least have got the full story from Demetriou before losing his temper. He chose to ignore the telling off 'what do you think we should do about Illianov?' he was dreading this part of the conversation, recalling the very clear instruction he had received to keep the man safe at all costs.

'We don't need to do anything Roman. The man got himself killed'.

Targ shook, what did she just say? 'What do you mean maam?'

'Our intelligence identified that he made an unprotected call last week to his mother. We don't know why as he always uses an encrypted handset that we supplied him with. Anyway, he made the call, someone obviously traced it and now he's paid the price.'

'So, it wasn't our fault then' the relief in his voice was audible.

'Will that be all Roman, I have another call to take'.

The phone went dead and Targ slumped back into his chair. He felt like he had no clue what was happening anymore, but it was ok, as his job appeared safe again.

Chapter 19

De Cathay appeared to be full of good spirits when he bumped into Paul Hindle in one of the many chapels on the first floor. 'Paul, I wanted to catch-up with you personally'.

Paul studied the huge man's frame and decided it was safe to engage 'ah Georges, how nice to see you again. I caught up with your man in Kos the other day and he gave me a good update'.

Georges wasn't at all surprised that Hindle had already found out who the man was and how to get in contact with him 'yes, he told me you'd been in touch. Good work all round I'd say.'

Paul recognised a smile and thought that was the first time he'd seen Georges so relaxed in along time. He decided not to divulge that the mission had in fact failed, that was for another day.

'The real reason I wanted to catch you is to thank you for arranging my Friday afternoon', De Cathay sneered as only he could.

'Glad to be of assistance' Paul responded flatly. He didn't really approve and thought De Cathay was taking a massive risk but, it was another thing in his armoury should he ever need protection.

'Yes indeed, she was perfect in every way, I hope we are paying her well?'

'Very well Georges.' Paul paused and recalled how much it cost to pay for her and her flights as well as the fee to his friend Roger Barlow for organising it all. 'I'm glad that you were err…satisfied'. Both men chuckled at Pauls play on words, walking away in opposite directions.

Later that day, Paul shuffled through the corridors quickly, his cassock billowing as he strode, sweat beading on his forehead. He knocked on the huge, panelled door just under the large brass plaque proclaiming the occupant to be 'Eduardo Musso', nothing else as no-one who didn't know what his role was, needed to know. The door was opened and the woman holding the door handle beckoned Paul inside. From across the room, Musso stood from his seat 'Ha ha, Cardinal Hindle, come in' Paul wasn't used to his colleagues addressing him so formally.

'Eduardo how are you' he stepped in tentatively and looked at the attractive lady who was now stood next to him.

'Paul meet Carla Perez; she is Alberto's replacement and started with us this week'.

Hindle turned slightly and offered his hand 'I'm Paul Hindle, head of security.

Congratulations Carla and welcome, I hope your role is successful' the words were genuine, and he smiled as they shook hands.

'Thank you Cardinal Hindle, I have heard much about you and it's a pleasure to meet you at last'.

'It's just Paul, we don't do the ceremonial stuff out of the public gaze'.

'Carla is having a first look at our financial position Paul so she may call on you for some input from time to time' Musso interjected.

'That is fine,' Paul responded directly to his new colleague 'just ask whatever and whenever you need, remember there are no formalities, I'm always available'. Paul knew that he needed to foster a close relationship with the new Head of Financial Affairs, especially as she was clearly a close ally of Musso. He also knew that he needed to start work on digging into her background as knowledge is power, especially if that knowledge included some indiscretions.

Musso walked over towards the two and addressed his new recruit 'there you go, well I'm glad you two have met now. Carla, I'll leave you to finish off your initial report. If you can get it to me by the weekend, I'd be grateful'. He shook hands with her and opened the door. Returning to his desk he looked up at Paul 'come, sit down.' His open hand gestured to the large, ornate wooden chair that sat across the equally extravagant desk. 'I thought that some of our recent conversations have been a bit difficult Paul, so I thought that rather than bark down the phone at you, we could have a more civil meeting, face to face, and perhaps get to the bottom of a few things. Americano?' he enquired.

'Perfect thanks' Paul replied unsure about what the next few minutes had in store for him. 'I'm always happy to spend time with you Eduardo, you know that'. Paul's wide eyes gave away the lie, but he hoped Musso hadn't noticed.

'What do you think of Carla?' Musso probed as he placed the cup of steaming black coffee on a coaster in front of Hindle.

'She seems very capable; I think we'll get on well. She's a lot younger than Alberto, so I'd imagine we'll miss a bit of his experience, but the new ways of thinking, especially around technology should benefit us'. Paul took a sip of his coffee, purposefully avoiding the gender point and waiting to see if his assessment was well received.

'Indeed Paul, Carla will be a great asset, you must get to know her and use her skills and knowledge wisely.'

Hindle acknowledged the comment with a nod and smiled. 'So, what can I do for you today, Eduardo?' He decided to get straight to the point and find out what was on Musso's mind, good or bad.

'I need us to work closer Paul. I'm a bit bothered that I don't know enough about your work and the significant benefits you bring to this place, so I thought we should get together more regularly, and this is the first of what I hope can be a positive experience for both of us.'

Hindle's mind was racing, Musso didn't do anything without good reason, and he didn't feel comfortable being this close to the firing line. 'I'm flattered that you of all people should take a close interest Eduardo, and obviously, I'm happy to support that'.

'For example, let me ask you a question'. Musso drank from his cup slowly, his voice was carefully measured, and his gaze never left Paul's. 'Why would the Vatican have a relationship with two Germans who currently reside in Brazil?'

The question nearly knocked Paul off his seat, and Musso saw the reaction. 'It's ok don't answer that. Two German citizens have been arrested in Brazil, accused of travelling on false passports. My contact over there seems to think that there is a link back to this building, but I have no knowledge of that, so I am sure it isn't true.' Musso paused for effect before continuing 'As head of security Paul, I'd expect you to be aware of this and make sure that any roads that might lead back to Rome from it are well and truly closed'. He stopped again and allowed Paul to respond.

At least he now knew why he'd not got a response from the German couple to his recent calls. 'I'll look into it and come back to you'.

'No, that won't be necessary Paul. I understand that some unsavoury things happen in the world that conflict with our way of life. I also understand that somewhere within these walls, some people know about such things. It is not for me to question those people or events internally, but I need to make sure that His Holiness is protected from them, and his integrity is not compromised in any way. So, if our Head of Security tells me that we have nothing to be concerned about, I am happy.

Paul was shocked at both the news about the Germans and Musso's acceptance that he somehow had a controlling influence in such matters. 'I'm sure that we have nothing to be worried about'.

'Good so I'll consider that particular item off my agenda'. Musso smiled again and Paul remained unsettled. 'Now, we have a problem.'

Paul's stomach churned, here was the real reason he had been summoned.

'Carla has done a quick review of our financial position and has raised two alarming things to me. Firstly, monies are being misappropriated through what appears to be Georges' office. I haven't yet got the full details, but significant and regular monthly amounts are disappearing from our central bank facility and the trail is ending up at De Cathay. There could be an easy explanation, but I doubt it.'

'Why would you trust me with this information?' Paul enquired nervously.

'Because you are Head of Security and I suspect that embezzlement falls under your remit. I want you to work quickly with Carla to establish the facts and tell me what's going on and what we're going to do about it'.

Paul felt his heart beating but tried hard to remain composed. 'Of course, Eduardo, I'll do whatever is necessary'.

'Also,' Musso came back without acknowledging the response 'these rumours about the attempted murder of Neerdorf are too close for comfort'.

Paul recognised the word 'attempted' and wondered what Musso knew. Before he could respond though Musso added 'its probably appropriate that we bring the arrangement with Neerdorf Securities to a close and we'll find another financier, if we need one at all. The repayment agreement is one of our largest single monthly commitments and our own banking house thinks it's unnecessary.'

'They sanctioned the deal when it was done though Eduardo' Paul retorted

'Well, that might be so, but the paperwork is apparently unclear, and the Head of our bank is not happy with it. You can manage the runoff and Carla can head up the re-arrangement, should it be required.'

Paul sat stunned but accepted the assignment 'I'll book some time in with Carla and we'll get onto it immediately'.

'Thank you, Paul. I think a weekly catch-up from hereon in feels like the way forward, so we can keep each other abreast of developments. It's good to collaborate Paul, don't you think?' The question seemed to be his cue to leave. 'Yes Eduardo, I'll put some dates in the diary'. Paul stood to leave.

'Don't worry yourself with that, I've already arranged it.' Musso stood and smiled 'just before you go Paul, what do you know about a prostitute visiting our chambers?'

Hindle turned and almost fell back into the chair 'a…a prostitute?' he felt the heat in his face rising and the sweat building in his palms.

'Again, I don't need you to answer, just know that there is young…lady' he chose his words carefully 'claiming to have visited a senior Cardinal last week in the Vatican. She is offering her story to the press for a significant sum. It goes without saying that such a story has the potential to do us a lot of harm.'

'I'll err look into it…'

'Do better than that Paul, close it down' with that Musso turned and walked back to the window that looked out over the lawns. He smiled to himself, happy that for once he seemed to be ahead of the curve as far as De Cathay and his unsavoury activities were concerned. He had made a commitment to himself to quickly resolve the unique problems that the overly aggressive Cardinal created and had left in his wake for so long. Now he was confident that another high-profile office was helping, that pledge was a step nearer to becoming a reality. Paul stood and made a swift exit, closing the door quietly, he felt the need to stop and steady himself, hand against the wall he gulped in deep breaths as he tried to bring his heart rate under control.

Alexis hadn't slept much, and it showed as he drove the short distance between his home and the station. His brain had been churning over the events of the previous day and he hadn't been able to switch off. There were too many questions about the Neerdorf case that had been overlooked, left unanswered or simply not recognised. He was deeply upset and concerned about the apparent assassination of a man he had legitimately interviewed just a few days earlier and he was confused and getting increasingly annoyed at the rush to close down the investigation that had held so much promise for his own future prospects. He was now trundling towards an unknown fate and felt a dread that he had never experienced before. In the next hour, it was entirely possible that he might find himself removed from his dream job and a career he had lived for all of his life. The worst thing about that was that he had no idea how it had come to this position, he had always done his very best and acted in the best interests of the force but now, here on this idyllic island, someone, somewhere appeared to be trying to destroy his ambitions and his life.

After parking his car in the usual spot, he walked into the station and was greeted by two of his colleagues, both of whom were smirking at him and making feigned vomiting noises. One of them held out a sick bag 'morning Demetriou' he laughed 'just in case your stomach can't manage it today'.
Alexis smiled remembering the mess he had made on the beach 'leave it out guys, I've got to go and see the boss. Is he in yet?'
Both nodded and pointed comically towards Targ's closed office door 'he seemed to be in a better mood today. Good luck.'
As he approached the door, it was opened from inside and Targ appeared. He looked his usual bedraggled, hassled self, grim faced and sporting unkempt straggly dark hair. 'Come in and grab yourself a coffee, I'll be a few minutes.' His demeanour giving nothing away about the way the meeting was to go, he walked off with a folder under his arm towards the front desk.
Alexis did as he was told and prepared a strong americano from the machine behind Targ's desk. He sat and sipped at it, stomach churning, head pounding, his nerves starting to build. What would he do if he were to be sacked, where could he go, who would be willing to employ him….The door opened and Targ entered, Alexis noticed he was without the folder. 'Right Demetriou, I've thought about what you had to say yesterday and whilst I don't condone your insubordination, I am on this occasion willing to let it go.' Alexis looked up from his crouched position, shoulders relaxing as he took in the words. 'I do however want this Neerdorf investigation closed properly and quickly. I have a task for you that will help with that.' He paused and took a drink from his off-white stained mug and sat down. 'I know

that Neerdorf met with two senior members of the Vatican finance office in the days before his accident. I would like to know what that meeting was about and how it concluded.'

'I can ask the Neerdorf's if they know anything sir…'

'No Demetriou' Targ interjected swiftly 'I would like you to go and see the Cardinals and get their version so we can shut this matter down once and for all'.

'In Rome sir?' Alexis was shocked at this development but was now even more confused than ever.

'Yes, I've arranged for you to see the two men concerned. HQ have sanctioned the flights you can pick the tickets up at the airport. You fly out tomorrow so use the rest of today to prepare and stay away from the Dutch family.'

Alexis sat clutching his hot cup, he felt the heat burning his hands, but it stopped him from shaking.

'That's all Demetriou, report back to me directly as soon as you get back.'

Alexis stood and walked out of the office in a daze. He turned as he opened the door 'what is our situation regarding Illianov sir?' his voice low and croaked through the dry nervousness that had overtaken him.

'Ah yes, the other mess. Well once again Demetriou, I have gone out of my way and put my neck on the line to clear that up for you and protect the reputation of this station.' Targ revelled in the self-glorification. 'Consider it sorted, we were not involved, in any way…understand?'

Alexis didn't but said 'yes'. He closed the door and felt the relief flow from his body.

Chapter 20

Paul Hindle got back to his office and found a handwritten post-it note stuck to monitor of his PC. 'Come to my office immediately' the note in De Cathays handwriting sent a ripple of nausea through Paul's stomach and head. He poured a glass of water from the bottle of Pellegrino in the cooler and sat in his chair, taking a long draught from the tall glass he tried to steady his nerves and clear his thoughts. He couldn't ever recall in all his many years, when so many things under his control where under so much challenge. It wasn't that he couldn't handle it, the stress came with the reasonably well-paid position he held, and the conflict was something that he had always relished, but something was happening that he wasn't comfortable with. It was the uncertainty around the politics that bothered him most, he could sense a shift in the power base, and he could see that Musso in particular was making a move to strengthen his position. The fact that he, Paul, was generally seen to be a supporter of, and was being supported by De Cathay placed him in a potentially vulnerable position, should Musso emerge as the victor in this battle. That said, Musso had, he thought, offered him an olive branch and Paul needed to consider very carefully how he managed that. A short rap on the door stirred him from his thoughts and before he had chance to respond it opened and De Cathay entered with a sense of urgency. 'Paul, did you not get my note?' his voice was rasping and breathless.

'Georges, yes I was just catching my breath and was going to find you'.

'Never mind, I'm here now. So, what do you know?'.

Paul was instantly on edge, how was he going to answer that widely open question. He decided to raise an alert that Musso was on the warpath. 'I was summoned to Eduardo's office to meet Alberto's replacement'.

'And what did you think of Carla Perez?'

'She seemed very capable' Paul responded cautiously.

'Capable of doing us some harm?'

Paul was expecting the question, understanding what Georges would be thinking. 'She knows what she's doing, that's for sure. Have you met her yet?

'No, I have given her an hour tomorrow. Anyway, its not her I am here about. Paul, did you know that Neerdorf is alive? Not only that but he's recovering quickly.' The tension in his face was clearly showing.

'Musso told me earlier' Paul decided not to answer the direct question. 'It is a shock Georges, and we need to think about how we complete the job properly'.

Georges reacted with fury 'this was your job, Paul; you were tasked with completing this task and covering the tracks. Not only have you failed but now everyone is all over it. Did you also know that Musso has sanctioned an interview with the Police investigating the matter? Eh Paul?' De Cathay prompted aggressively, stabbing his finger at Pauls face.

'Georges, you need to calm down. Shouting at me solves nothing...'

'DON'T TELL ME TO CALM DOWN! We are in the shit here my friend, and we need to clean it up, very quickly, do you UNDERSTAND?'

Paul, steadied himself, it had been a while since he'd seen the Head of Legal Practice in such a state. The bigger problem was that this was just one thing, how would he react when he found out about the other things on Musso's 'to-do' list. 'Georges, we've had difficulties to manage in the past and we always find a way. I didn't know about the police interview but what can they know? At least our tracks are completely covered. It will be ok and Neerdorf will be sorted.' Paul relaxed a little as he watched De Cathays shoulders soften under his cassock.

Georges sat in the chair opposite Paul. He looked more stressed than Hindle had ever seen him 'there is something else Paul'.

'Go on Georges, what is it?'

'The girl that you arranged last week is trying to blackmail us.'

Paul again decided to keep his knowledge to himself, allowing Georges to construe the silence as shock or surprise or anything else he felt might be appropriate.

'Apparently she's trying to sell her story to the TV news agencies.' He sat in his seat, agitated but holding on to his rage. 'Where did you get her from Paul?'

Hindle tensed 'she is from our usual source Georges. I will ask our contact to silence her, one way or another.'

'But we know that using third parties is becoming unreliable.' Georges hissed through clenched teeth. We need to use our most trusted people, Paul. YOU' he raised his voice 'need to make sure she is removed and cannot do us any harm'.

'Our problem here Georges is that we can't just have her killed…'

'Yes, we can, and quickly' De Cathays voice was becoming hard, almost evil.

'Georges, we can't just exterminate everyone who falls out with us, and besides, she has contacts now with the News Agencies, if she disappears now, they'll be all over the story and us…you'. Paul waited to see how De Cathar responded. There was silence as that truth sank in. 'This is all about money Georges, I'll make contact and pay her off and then arrange to send her away somewhere out of the way for a year or so.'

'Quickly and quietly Paul. I don't need Musso questioning me about this any further.'

'I'll get on to it immediately and then I'll get something done about our Dutch friend.'

'Leave Neerdorf until we've seen the police officer tomorrow. We need to know what they know, ok?'

'That's a good strategy Georges, yes.'

'Any other problems I need to know about?'

'None that I am aware of' Paul lied. He thought that he'd see what Carla knew or was thinking before he approached Georges about the missing money and the movement of the draw down facility'.

'Keep me up to date please'. De Cathay stood and moved towards the door 'I'm very troubled Paul, I can sense trouble like a boil on my arse. Let's nip this in the bud and make sure it doesn't get even further out of hand. We both stand to lose an awful lot; we need to stay together'. He exited as quickly as he had entered and closed the door firmly behind him.

Paul sat and contemplated what had happened and what had been said by both senior Cardinals. He desperately wanted to help De Cathay get out of the tangled mess that was starting to envelop him but also, he anxiously needed to keep on the right side of Musso. His well-honed political artistry was clearly needed as he carefully considered his next moves. Within the hour he was on the phone to Roger Barlow, discussing the girl he had selected and sent last week to fulfil the regular service that had taken place over the past few years. Paul had to remember that until now, the service had delivered and had always been discreet. Not just that, but Roger was a key part of Paul's network and continued to have a great value, so he needed to handle this with great care. 'No-one is blaming you Roger, but we need to sort this out as its clearly gathering momentum'.

Roger sat in his office, surrounded by pungent cigarette smoke. 'What are you thinking Paul?'

'De Cathay suggests that we get rid of her' Paul disclosed 'but I'm not sure that is wise given the closeness of the press. I think a financial incentive might be better'.

'Financial? In what way?' Roger's heart began to sink at the thought that he might have to dig into his pocket.

'We need to find out how much she is selling the story for and then you need to double it'. Paul thought he'd try and get a contribution from his friend.

'And you want me to fund that?' Roger retorted, getting angry. 'In the whole time we have known each other Paul, have I ever let you down? Ever?'

'Roger, take it easy…'

'Answer me Paul, have I ever let you down?'

Paul remained quiet for a few seconds 'no, you haven't and that is why I'm trying to work with you to sort this out'.

'Well, it doesn't feel that way. I can't just find two hundred thousand euro's…'

'So, you know what she's wants…'

'Paul, it's my business to know what is happening over here and besides, I know one of the journalists who approached me to be a go between just yesterday'.

'Ok, so we need to find 200,000 euros to make this go away.' It was a statement rather than a question. It was also significantly cheaper than he was expecting which made the conversation easier to manage. 'OK Roger I can see how difficult it is for you, I'll put that funding in place on one condition.'

'Go on' Roger eased a bit.

'You need to send her away. Can you use that apartment you own in Phuket and get her to lay low for a year or so?'

'Jesus Paul, I use that as a retreat' he thought for a while and deduced that this was as good as it was going to get. 'Ok yes, you provide the cash and an airline ticket to Thailand, and I'll get her to the apartment. I'll also encourage her to withdraw any comments she's made to the press so it's clean.'

Job done; Paul was happier that one of his issues looked like it was easier to resolve than he at first thought. Now for the other tasks, starting with preparing for the investigating officer from Greece.

Chapter 21

Hindle landed in Rome's Fiumicino airport after a short and comfortable flight. It was easy for him to get a cab given the steady, flowing stream of bright white vehicles filtering past the arrivals exit and the drive to his hotel was a good one, even though the traffic was heavy and stop, start. He found the driver engaging and knowledgeable about the city which would be a help when he was seeing the sights this evening, ahead of his meeting in the morning. He had his plan worked out and was happy that he had the questions ready to capture all the information he needed to establish how and why the Vatican had a link with a little-known finance house from the Netherlands and what that relationship meant to the running of arguably the largest and most important institution on the planet.

After a very acceptable, early dinner in the hotel restaurant, Alexis decided to take a walk in the still warm, evening sunshine and take in a few of the historical sights on the Eastern side of the river where he had based himself. He had already plotted his route for the morning and knew that he would need to cross the Pont Cavour to get to the walled city but for now, he was comfortable walking in the opposite direction, aiming to find the Trevi Fountain and take in the crowds and atmosphere of this beautiful and ancient place. The buildings and architecture astounded him, and the hustle and bustle was exciting bordering on intimidating for someone used to the pedestrian lifestyle of his tiny island in Greece. He found himself carried along with the flow and pace of the various tourist groups and he was able to latch on to a guided tour that was moving at a reasonable pace along the roads and going in his general direction. Stopping to listen to the tour guide talk about the Colonna Di Marco Aurelio, Alexis became aware of a movement in the crowd as someone appeared to be pressing through it towards him. The throng of people ahead of him jostled and parted and he felt himself moving with the momentum. A strange sense of danger washed over him as he became less in control of his movements; the crowd was definitely reacting to some hostility as it resisted then gave way to whatever force was moving its way through. He caught sight of a thick set man, with dark hair and beard, his face contorted with what looked like anger and rage getting closer to him, aggressively pushing the tourists that now enveloped Alexis, out of his way. Demetriou tried unsuccessfully to get out of the way, he turned to move away from the oncoming force but the crowd, which was now swelling with onlookers, curious to see what the commotion was, stood firmly in his path. He thought he heard his name being called but surely not, no one outside of the Vatican knew about his visit. 'Demetriou!' It was there again, loudly shouted this time and before he had time to react the man was in front of him, invading his already closed in personal space. The bearded face was literally an inch from his own, he could smell the acrid breath of his aggressor and the strong body odour pouring off his body. 'Who are you?' Alexis shouted over the din of the crowd.

'Follow me, I need to speak with you'. The mysterious man moved past Alexis creating a gap for him to follow. As they got to the exterior of the huge crowd, the man waited for Alexis, grasped his arm, and marched him into a side road off the Via del Corso where it was almost deserted and more importantly quiet. Alexis stood, alarmed, and shocked, 'what is going on here, who are you?' his eyes wide and his heart thumping.

'Who I am doesn't matter. I have a message for you Mr Demetriou. You have a meeting tomorrow morning with a representative of the Catholic Church'.

'How do you know that?' Alexis couldn't believe what he was hearing.

The heavy-set man was breathing heavily and sweating profusely 'I am paid to know. One of the men you will meet is called Cardinal De Cathay, you need to be careful with him. He is a dangerous man and has a history that is the antithesis of everything he preaches. Do not take everything he tells you to be the truth and be sure to ask him about his relationship with the Governor of the bank on your island and the Chief of Police here in Rome.'

'Wait, just slow down. I need to know who you are and what your interest is in this matter' Alexis remained shaken but managed to steady himself enough to appear steady.

'you're close to opening up something big Demetriou, but be careful, watch your back'.

A black BMW screeched to a halt behind Alexis and the back door sprang open. As he turned to look what else what was happening the man ran towards to it and dived into the back seat. The car took off before the door was closed, turning quickly left it disappeared into the depths of the city. Alexis stood in disbelief, becoming aware of his own gasping breaths and heavy perspiration, he stood letting the coolness of the night air waft over him. 'What the hell was that all about' he said aloud, to himself. From his position of the corner of the street he spotted a taxi heading in his direction, 'for hire' clearly lit in orange on its roof. Time to go back to the hotel, he thought.

The occupant in the back of the black BMW made a call as soon as he got his breath back 'It took me a while, but I found him and delivered the message. I've left him on the corner of Via Del Corso and our taxi is on its way to pick him up and take him safely back to the hotel.' No more words were spoken, and the phone went dead.

In his office deep inside the Vatican, Eduardo Musso placed his mobile phone back in his drawer, took a long sip of his Montepulciano D'Abruzzo and sat in his ornate seat with a contented smile. He could sense that Cardinal De Cathay was on the back foot and his days as a senior member of the church were numbered.

Alexis arrived back at his hotel room a little shaken from his experience but thankful that he was safe and unharmed. Recounting the events of the last hour in his mind he failed to come up with a rationale for the message and the way it was delivered, surely if someone wanted to speak with him, all they had to do was come and find him at the hotel. Another thing struck him as he was thinking; the taxi driver knew where he was going, and he drove off before taking payment. The evening was getting more and more strange! Putting the strangeness aside, he made sure to make a physical note on his interview sheet, to ask the Cardinal about his relationships with the bank, the police and the Neerdorf family but then he thought, if they were all linked in some way, and they all led back to the Vatican…what on earth was he about to find out and what danger might that put him in. Alexis tried hard to put it out of his mind so he could get some sleep, but that never happened, and he spent most of the night turning mentally and physically, losing the irony that he was in the most comfortable bed he had been in for years.

Thomas Neerdorf entered the hospital to be greeted by the Chief Medical Officer he had met with his brother. 'Mr Neerdorf, hello how nice to see you'.

The pleasant welcome took Thomas a little by surprise but made his feel good 'Hello Dr McKeown, thank you. How are things today?'

'Well, we have news. Your father is responding well to treatment, and we are considering bringing him out of the coma later today or tomorrow morning, all being well. Good news I think you'll agree?'

Thomas felt relief and couldn't hide the delight as a broad smile appeared across his face 'that is fantastic news yes, when will you know for sure?'

'We need to undertake a few more tests and follow their results closely first, then we'll have an accurate idea' the doctor expertly avoided the question. 'You can see him now Thomas but if you can ask your family to leave visiting tomorrow whilst we assess his condition, I will give you a call when I have a clear view.'

'That sounds reasonable Doctor, thank you.' Thomas turned and entered his fathers' room, taking the seat next to his bed he looked at the myriad of wires, tubes and screens and closed his eyes, silently praying that his father might have some answers to the mysteries that surrounded him and the business and hoping desperately that the missing cash could be accounted for. He couldn't help feeling that wouldn't be the case however, and there was still a long way and a lot of work to do before they could get anywhere near to the bottom of what had taken place on the dreadful day. Thomas looked at his dad and held his hand. He looked peaceful and felt warm, Thomas was almost sorry that by this time tomorrow, the peace and warmth he was looking at, would be shattered as the CEO of Neerdorf Securities became aware of how close he had been to death and how near, the business he had worked all his life to build, came to closing.

Chapter 22

The telephone in the room woke Alexis with a start. After a long night of drifting in and out of sleep, he had spent the last hour in a deep slumber and felt awful as he reached for the phone. The automated alarm notified him that it was 7 am. He reluctantly crawled out from under the duvet and headed for the shower before getting dressed and making his way to the dining room for breakfast of a strong black coffee and two warm croissants. As he sat at his table for one, casually and self-consciously reading the morning newspaper he hadn't noticed the Maître D' make a quick call 'he is down for breakfast now and his bags are stored in the safe room as he's returning to pick them up after his meeting. I would guess he is leaving for that shortly. Yes, I'll call you when he leaves.'
Hindle put the phone down and called through to the Vatican concierge services and arranged for a car to be available to pick Alexis up from the hotel and then for coffee to be delivered to the meeting room as soon as their guest arrived.

The black BMW waiting for him was a nice surprise, but it sparked a vivid memory of the crazy messenger from the night before. Putting that aside he relaxed in the wonderfully comfortable rear seat as he prepared himself for the meeting as best he could. Taking in the magnificent sights that surrounded him as the driver expertly manoeuvred through the creeping traffic and uncompromising one-way system. They glided over the bridge and passed the two police stations before getting on to Via Cresenzio, turning right at St Peters Square and following the arc of the road until they finally turned off into a private drive. The car came to a stop and the door was immediately opened by a man in the Swiss Guards uniform 'Buongiorno Senor Demetriou, follow me please and I'll escort you to your meeting'.
Alexis, impressed by the efficiency of the greeting climbed out of the car, thanking both the driver and the guard as he continued to follow in through the huge and majestic entrance. The buildings in this part of Rome dated back as early and the 3rd and 4th centuries, some having been restored like this one around the 1500's, but all of them looking magnificent and regal, revealing the splendour and projecting the mysticism and glory attached to the history of Rome, Vatican City and the Catholic Church. Alexis was in awe of his surroundings, and he just wanted to stop, look around and take it all in but of course, he was here on business and his escort was making good progress through the corridors, so he needed to concentrate and keep up with the pace. They walked across an open lobby and off to the left was a narrower corridor which stopped at a large double door. As with everything he'd seen so far it was opulently decorated with carved swirls and was adorned with heavy brass furniture. The guard opened one of the doors and stood inside announcing 'officer Demetriou your Eminence', then stepping away to allow Alexis through and into the room. As he did so, he was immediately met by the outstretched hand of a man dressed in black trousers and clerical shirt with tab collar. 'Welcome to Vatican City Alexis, I'm Cardinal Hindle, you can call me Paul'.
Alexis took the hand and shook it warmly; it was a soft hand he felt but the grip was as strong as iron and as he looked into the face of the man greeting him, he noticed a strong steely stare from bright crystal-clear eyes. 'Thank you I'm incredibly happy to be here and thank you for your time, I appreciate it.' Alexis looked over Paul's shoulder and saw the massive frame of another Cardinal moving towards the pair of them. This one was in full cassock and sporting

a heavy gold coloured crucifix on a strong large, linked chain. Apart from that nothing about his look or demeanour suggested anything pious. This must be the one I was warned about he thought to himself. The two made eye contact and De Cathay introduced himself 'come sit down, let us take a coffee and we can get started on your agenda'. Paul poured the drinks and placed a cup of steaming hot black liquid in front of Alexis, 'milk, cream and sugar is on the table, please help yourself', and he took a seat across the table next to his colleague. Despite the pleasantries Alexis felt a tension in the air that made him more nervous than he was used to. It took him a little by surprise and as he took hold of the coffee cup it rattled in the saucer as his fingers trembled.

'Right' De Cathay was hoping this was going to be quick 'how can we help you Officer Demetriou?'

That's an end to the niceties Alexis thought to himself. He smiled as he looked across at the two gentlemen opposite 'I'm the investigating officer looking into a serious incident at a hotel in Kos involving a guest who I understand, is known to you?

'Yes, we heard about that' De Cathay responded with an empathy in voice 'such a tragic accident, it is such a shame for his wife and sons, to have lost their husband and father in such circumstances. We can only hope he receives peace in heaven and that his family find solace in God.' Georges looked over at Alexis and gave him a surprisingly saintly smile. Alexis noted that Georges eyes remained dark and cold, however. He glanced fleetingly at Cardinal Hindle and thought he sensed the man flinch as he listened to the words being spoken.

'Thankfully, it's not a murder enquiry Cardinal' Alexis corrected the assumption 'but Mr Neerdorf is in a critical condition at the moment.'

De Cathay was stunned but remained controlled. He gave Hindle a questioning look which set the hairs on Paul's neck on end. 'Ah, I have been misinformed, my mistake. We obviously, in that case wish the man well and hope for a speedy recovery. So, what might this have to do with the Catholic Church?' De Cathay recovered from his shock well.

'I understand Cardinal, that the firm Mr Neerdorf represents has a financial arrangement with the Church…'

De Cathay interrupted the flow of Alexis' question 'that may or may not be the case. Such things are conducted in a most confidential matter, you know that Mr Demetriou' he placed an aggressive emphasis was on the salutation. 'Only the finance house can confirm what business arrangements they are facilitating'.

Alexis was feeling on the back foot and sensed the atmosphere tighten. 'I have spoken with the Neerdorf family, and I have details of a cash transaction that took place here in Vatican City just days before the accident at the hotel' he tried to avoid making any untruths.

'Which one of the Neerdorf's?' Paul decided he should take some control over proceedings before Georges allowed his frustrations to get the better of him. 'And what sort of cash transaction?'

'I've spoken with the other two directors of the finance house'.

Paul sensed that the man opposite didn't have much, if anything to go on, 'we haven't met either of them. What exactly are they saying about a 'cash transaction', do you think the Catholic Church is in the habit of working in cash?' Hindle let out a small snigger.

Alexis carried on unperturbed, 'they are claiming that a significant amount of cash has gone missing, and the day before it went missing, their father had the fall. They have suggested that the two things might be connected.'

De Cathay laughed loudly 'are you making this up?' He looked at Hindle 'this is starting to sound like a bad film script'. Georges let the atmosphere settle and looked directly at Alexis 'have you fully investigated these allegations before coming to waste our time, Officer?'

Alexis visibly stiffened 'I need to make sure I close off all avenues properly Cardinal. I don't see this as a waste of time, I simply need to ask you the relevant questions and then cross you off the list.'

'Listen to yourself' Georges retorted. 'What is this large amount of cash'.

Alexis wondered whether to divulge the amount. He chose to ignore the question 'can I ask you about your relationship with the Cullis Vaults private bank on Kos' He looked directly at De Cathay.

Both Cardinals looked at each other and Paul decided it was best if he responded. 'We don't know what you're talking about. Why would we have a relationship with a small private bank on a small insignificant Greek island. Nothing you are saying makes any sense.'

'Ok' Alexis made a note on his laptop of the transcript. 'The Chief of Police sends his regards by the way'.

'Enough!' De Cathay stood up and looking down at Alexis said calmly 'you dare to threaten us by namedropping the Chief of Police. This is a joke; you, are a joke.' There was short silence as all three men captured their own individual thoughts. 'So, on a small island in the Greek Aegean Sea, there has been the theft of a large amount of cash and an attempted murder. I think that is what you are suggesting?' De Cathay pressed on. 'That must take a lot of resource to fully investigate. How big a team are you in charge of?'

Alexis looked up into the huge face that leered down on him. 'I'm the investigating officer and actually, I'm working the case on my own at the moment'.

'So, your superiors don't think there is sufficient reason to open this matter up to a full investigating team?' Paul's question struck Alexis right between the eyes.

Georges jumped in, 'It looks to me like you're here on a whim then. You have no evidence of a theft or come to that an attempt to murder anyone. Like I said this is a waste of time.'

Hindle put his head down unsure where Georges was going.

Alexis steadied himself, 'so you have no dealings with the bank then?' he wanted to press the point as he suspected that he'd hit a nerve, irrespective of the initial denial.

'We have our own banking facility Mr Demetriou' Paul's response was measured and calm 'here in this fine City. We might use other specialist finance routes from time to time, but we would not have dealings with an institution that resided in a state with a such poor credit rating.'

Alexis almost the felt the verbal slap in the face. It was time to delve deeper into the missing cash, 'I'm curious as to why Mr Neerdorf would have the need to collect five million dollars from you both'. He left the statement open and watched for a reaction.

'That is a large amount of cash' De Cathay was first to respond. 'Has Mr Neerdorf actually confirmed this?'

The officer was on the spot now, he knew that Neerdorf had been in a coma since the accident, and he knew that the Cardinals both knew Neerdorf hadn't been in a position to make any comments. 'Not exactly…'

De Cathay held up his hand, halting Alexis' response. 'No evidence of a theft, no evidence of an attempted murder, no evidence of any actual cash being missing. Let me ask you this Alexis Demetriou,' Georges paused for effect watching the policeman sweat, 'exactly why have you come here today and upon whose instruction? I ask because the more you speak, the more idiotic and juvenile you sound.'

Alexis sat feeling isolated and out of his depth. His hands started to tremble slightly, and he felt beads of sweat running from his forehead and down the side of temples.

'I think our time is up' Paul offered a way out and both Cardinals stood.

'It was nice to see you Alexis' De Cathay lied, sneering as he made his way to the door. On his way out he pressed a button at the side of the door to summon the guard.

Paul walked around the table, 'we'll take you back to the hotel Alexis, the guard will be here in a second or two.'

Alexis shuffled his belongings back into his case and stood to shake hands. 'Thank you for your time, I'm sorry to have wasted it'. He spoke quietly and didn't make any attempt at eye contact.

'At least you can cross us of your list' Paul smiled and returned the handshake. 'Goodbye Alexis'. He turned and left the room just as the uniformed guard appeared and escorted him back to the black BMW.

Paul stopped off at De Cathays office and knocked on the door before entering without being invited. He slipped in quickly, closing the door behind him and taking a seat opposite Georges. 'What did you think about that?' Hindle asked.

Ignoring the question, De Cathay seethed 'fucking Neerdorf is alive? What the hell is going on?'

Paul sat in silence not knowing if it was really a question. 'We need to think about what we do with Neerdorf but first, he knows too much Paul' referring to the policeman and answering Paul's initial question, De Cathay sounded alarmed. 'But he has no support from his superiors and is clearly not clever enough to put it all together. That said, he makes me uncomfortable.' De Cathay sat firm in his seat, eyes fixed on Paul's waiting for a solution.

'I think we can let it lie Georges, the bank and the Greek police are on our side and even if the family press it, there are no doors open for them to get any information.' Paul knew as he spoke that De Cathay wasn't of the same mind.

'We should make sure that all avenues are indeed closed Paul and that includes making sure that this maverick junior officer can't cause us any more trouble.'

Hindle instinctively knew what was coming next but asked anyway. 'What does that mean Georges?'

'We must get rid of him' De Cathay spoke matter of fact, without any sign of emotion 'I've instructed our driver to take our little friend on a tour of the city then bring him back here to the underground vaults. We can dispose of him in the Tevere.'

Paul shook his head, 'Georges we have had this conversation before, we just can't eliminate everyone who disagrees with us…'

'I am aware of that Paulo and agree...to some extent. ' Georges used the Italian form of his name. He did it occasionally Paul noted, when Georges needed him on side. He used it to reinforce their Latin bond and the fact that they were both alien to the country that they lived and worked in. 'This man however has the capacity to upset a lot of people and create a problem that will damage us' he gestured, pointing his finger between them both, 'and that is something that we just can't allow to happen. I have it in hand Paulo, we just need to greet the policeman back in about an hour or so and then you need to have the right people arranged to do what is needed and make it look like an accident.'

Paul knew he wasn't going to win this one. 'What, within an hour?' he felt the stress building again and the thud in his chest began to beat faster. 'That might not happen Georges, it's a lot to organise in short a short space of time.' His voice was pleading but deep inside, he knew he just had no choice.

'I trust you Paulo, I know you can do what is required' Georges smiled and stood up, giving Paul his cue to leave. 'Be back here in 45 minutes Paul and we'll review your plan'. As he stood, Georges slid a mobile phone over to Paul. 'Look after this as well, its Demetriou's, he must have dropped it'.

Paul doubted that but said nothing. Taking the phone he left the room, breathing heavily and rapidly tried to turn things over in his mind. He got to his own office and slumped in his chair, leaning forward with his head in hands. For the first time in as long as he remembered, Paul Hindle was disliking his job and deplored the day he got so close to and involved with Georges De Cathay. At least his colleague now knew the truth about the state of the Dutchman, he could only dread what plan he had in his mind to close that particular problem off.

Chapter 23

Thomas received the call from Dawson McKeown just after breakfast. With a huge sense of relief, he organised Morgan to drive him and the other two members of the family to the hospital and they arrived within the hour. All three of them were in high spirits following the news that Neerdorf senior was awake and communicating, with a bit of effort, but speaking nonetheless and appearing to be compos mentis. Morgan dropped them at the entrance to the main reception area of the hospital, promising to return in an hour he then carried on with the car to fulfil another small errand he already had in the chauffeur business' diary. Thomas allowed his mother to enter the building, following her with Erik and as soon as they appeared, they were greeted by a tired looking Chief Medical Officer, dressed in smart grey suit, sparkling white shirt and eye-catching yellow tie, he approached the trio immediately and offered a wide smile and firm handshake. 'Welcome Mrs Neerdorf,' he addressed the mother instinctively given she was the senior member of the group. 'How very lovely to see you.' The charming smile hid his anxiety about how long her husband would remain able to see his family following his long unconscious state and also the threat to his life that potentially still existed following what he saw as an assassination attempt a few days earlier. 'Your husband is responding well, and we are incredibly pleased with his progress.' He altered his stance slightly so he could address all three visitors, 'When you go in to see him you must take account however that he is very tired, and you shouldn't get him stressed in any way. Also, don't be alarmed with the number of cables and tubes, we need to keep him in a high state of monitoring so we can react quickly if he starts to deteriorate.' Dawson smiled and gestured with his open hand that the way to the room was open. As the three entered the room, each of them looked eagerly at the patient for initial, hopefully positive signs, and they found happily that Dirk was already sat up albeit supported. The previously mentioned monitoring equipment buzzing, and beeping was however, an instant reminder that there was still a long way to go until full recovery was achieved. Katharine was the first to react, quickly moving to the side of the bed and throwing her arms around her husband, his eyes had immediately lit up when he saw his guests and now as he caught the scent of his wife, his they welled up as the emotion took hold of him. They all hugged and kissed him in turn, smiling and crying in equal measure before taking the seats that had been placed out ready for their arrival. 'What is like to be back dad' Erik's broad smile showed his bright white teeth 'we sure have missed you'.

Dirk responded in a rasping, laboured voice that took the family by surprise 'I'm so glad to see you all' he manged to say with the effort showing across his face 'what have you all been up to?'

Thomas looked across at his mother, her face was smiling but he could see that she was hurting behind her eyes. He was hoping for a sign from her about how much to tell his father, but it wasn't there 'we're glad to see you too dad, it's been a worrying time, but we can see you're as strong as an ox' he laughed gently but they could all see that Dirk was far from being as strong as anything. Thomas was desperate for information though, he needed to know what happened in that hotel and more importantly what had happened to the $5 million dollars his father had collected. 'How is your memory of what happened' he decided to gently prod, looking at Erik for some sort of approval.

Dirk closed his eyes for a moment, 'I don't think I have any recollection over what the nurse and surgeon told me'. His words came in short, sharp bursts, 'although I have had a few flash backs over the past week as I've been awakening. I don't know if they are accurate though or just recalling what I've been told'. He gave a long gasping breath and relaxed back into his pillow, his eyes again closing as he seemed to need time to recover after the effort of speaking.

Erik decided to join in. 'do you remember going to the bank before the hotel incident?' his voice was low and gentle, disguising the frantic nature of the enquiry and the fast-beating pulse he could feel pumping at his temples.

Dirk opened his eyes again, but the focus was way off into the distance, his breathing was deep and steady, but the monitor machine had increased its pace and with it the volume. The door opened and Dawson McKeown entered 'please, I must ask you to stop questioning the patient. It isn't good for him as I think you can hear'.

'Sorry doctor' Katharine leaned forward and took hold of Dirk's hand, 'we'll just sit for a while, if that's ok?' She looked sternly at both of her sons. 'I think it might be best if you two leave me here for a while, just while he settles down'. Without any more being said the men stood and left the room along with McKeown.

Erik was first to speak as they strode along the corridor to the visitors waiting room 'he's still bad isn't he doc?'

'I did say to you that he was far from being back to his old self, it will happen though, you just need to be patient.' Dawson addressed them both matter of fact 'can I get you a coffee?' They declined the offer of drinks and took a seat in the waiting room. It was a large open space with what looked like new furniture placed around it so family groups could gather and maintain some sort of respectful distance from anyone else who might be in there. There was a nice selection of free snacks, fruit, and drinks as well a bubbling coffee pot set on a table with a plentiful supply of cups, saucers, and cutlery. It was all very impressive and comfortable but as Erik had remarked, they were paying for it.

The black executive car sped out from the Vatican City walls and headed Southeast on the Via Della Lungara. The river looked calm and sparkled in the bright sun as the driver took a left across the Ponte Garibaldi and onto Rome's complex crossings of historical streets. Alexis sat and tried to watch the amazing views, but he just couldn't concentrate as the events of the morning were running around in his head. The meeting he had just attended didn't run anywhere near the way he had planned it and he couldn't fathom out how and why it had taken the turn that it did. His questions were the right ones to ask, he hadn't been overly aggressive in delivering them, he had maintained a calm and friendly approach throughout, yet the Cardinal's had reacted in a very hostile manner, the larger of the two in particular. The only conclusion Alexis could reach was that there was something to investigate further here, and that the Vatican was hiding something. How can that be though? How can the Roman Catholic Church, the bastion of everything that is good in the world, the institution of love and respect that holds all relationships in the highest esteem be complicit in such wrongdoing. It embodies truth and integrity and preaches respect and deliverance from evil. Holiness, virtue, Godliness. Yet here in the very epicentre of that culture Alexis had felt a coldness that chilled his heart and he had sat face to face with a man, De Cathay, who appeared to be more akin to the Devil than the Holy Spirit and all that envelops it and that his ancient, holy attire represented. Alexis was deeply concerned but he couldn't put a finger on what it was exactly. He mulled it all over in his mind, again and again. The messenger who had sought him out the evening before had warned him to be on his guard, but even after that strange encounter he couldn't have been ready for the short, sharp shock of a discussion he had experienced. The reaction to his suggestion that the Vatican had a working relationship with Cullis Vaults was extraordinary and led him to believe that the opposite to what the Cardinals had claimed was in fact the case. Similarly, the Chief of Police was naturally required to have contacts within the city walls, but De Cathay had virtually exploded when Alexis had mentioned it. None of it made any sense, unless there was a connection between them all that led back to the Neerdorf's. And, if that were the case then something deeply disturbing was taking place and the relative parties were doing all they could to keep a lid on it. A dangerous realisation crept out of that thinking and hit Alexis firmly between the eyes. If Alexis was close to uncovering something sinister, then he himself could be in danger. The thought shook him out his warm slumber in the back of the car. He looked around trying to establish where in Rome he was and how far from the hotel. As he looked out of the window the car slowed in the traffic and he realised that the building on his left was the Museo Nazionale Romano but why was he this far out, heading East. 'Where are we driver' he leaned forward to catch the ear of the uniformed guard at the wheel 'I need to be at the hotel if I'm to get back to the airport on time'.

'it's ok sir, the Cardinal Hindle has asked you to return to see them. It seems they have had a rethink following your earlier meeting and they would like the opportunity to revisit your agenda'.

'But what about my flight? I've paid for a return this afternoon!' Alexis was taken aback but knew he wouldn't be able to put a missed flight ticket on expenses.

'I understand that the Cardinal is arranging for the ticket to be switched to a later flight sir.' Alexis sat back, not sure what was going on. 'I need to make a call to my HQ to let them know I will be late then.' He reached into his bag for his mobile phone. It wasn't there, he was sure he had switched it off and put it in the zip pocket inside his file case. He held off the panic that was rising and his heart began to pump faster, 'where is my phone?' he asked aloud not necessarily addressing the driver 'I left here in my case...'.

'ah' the driver looked at him from the rear-view mirror, 'the Cardinal also said that you had dropped your phone in the meeting room. Apparently, it was on the floor under the seat you had occupied. We'll collect it shortly, sir'.

It felt wrong, the atmosphere in the car had changed and he could see that the driver himself was showing signs of stress. Alexis held onto his case firmly and stared out of the door window in silence, listening to the distant buzz of the car radio and the rapid growl of the traffic as the car sped up and slowed down in its flow. The car turned left and left again, obviously now making its way back towards the river, they approached the large roundabout at the Grand Hotel just as there was surge in vehicle volume, the driver entered the outside lane and indicated right, intending to cross the Via Torino. The moped rider came out of nowhere and at speed crashed into the front driver's side door, causing the airbag to activate and an alarm to sound inside the car. The moped fell alongside the heavily damaged BMW and its rider flew across the bonnet before crashing to floor with a sickening thud and squelch as his thin shirt was ripped from his torso exposing a bloodied body and buckled legs. Luckily, the helmet had protected his head but on first glance Alexis realised that the young boy was in a bad way. His initial instinct was to get out of the car and rush to attend the injured male, lying prone and twisted on the tarmac. As Alexis opened the car door, which had unlocked following the impact, he realised that the traffic had come to a halt and people were gathering quickly, some already offering help, calling for the emergency services and attending to the wounds. A quick glance at the driver's seat of the BMW showed the driver was trapped as the dent in the door had buckled the lock and hinge mechanism and as the driver fought unsuccessfully to try and wrestle the door open, the sirens appeared over the din in the distance. Without thinking about where he was going, Alexis walked quickly away reaching a clearing in the crowd he began to run along the pavement, following the Via Nazionale he took a random right turn into the smaller Via Genova which by pure chance brought him to a police station. He entered breathing heavily and holding out his Greek Police identification badge 'I need a phone urgently, please' the desk officer recognising the ID opened the side door and guided Alexis through into an office, empty apart from desk, chair, and landline telephone. Grabbing the handset, he punched numbers into the pad and waited. Nothing. He looked around for assistance, but the desk officer had disappeared. He tried again, slower this time but still nothing. The door opened and Alexis recognised the uniform of a Superintendent, 'Officer Demetriou I presume' she said as she strode into the room 'I think you are forgetting the international dialling code'.

Alexis felt foolish as the realisation sank in, but he also felt comforted at the mention of his name.

The Superintendent offered her hand 'I'm Gianna Sartori, we've been looking for you.'

They shook hands and Gianna explained that they'd had a call from his office on Kos earlier as they had been unable to make contact with him. She organised a coffee and allowed Alexis to recover from his unscheduled run before leaving him to make his call to the front desk at Kos. It was answered quickly enough by a familiar voice which relaxed him even more 'It's me Alexis, can you put me through to Targ immediately please.' The phone went quiet for just a few seconds.

'Alexis, where are you?' Targ's voice had a caring urgency about it 'we've been worried about you, what's going on?'

'Sir, I'm sorry but I think I'm in danger,'

'What do you mean?' Targ's tone changed.

'I've seen the Cardinals this morning and I think they are involved in something really bad.'

'Calm down Demetriou, take a breath. Remember this is the Vatican you are talking about and also that you are on an unprotected phone line.'

'Sir. They have stolen my phone and made me miss my flight,' he started to feel a bit exasperated.

'Alexis, listen to yourself. It's unthinkable that the Cardinals, of all people would steal your phone. What are you planning to do next and when can we expect you back in the office?'

'I need help going back to collect my phone and listen to what else they have to say, can you send someone please?' As he spoke the words, he knew that Targ didn't have the resources to make that happen and the dismissive manner in which his superior officer was reacting worried him.

'Alexis, I don't have anyone available at such short notice, but I will speak with my contact there in Rome and see if we can organise some support for you.'

That was better than nothing and at least he would have someone with him to witness the next exchange he was going to have with the Catholic Church. 'Thank you, sir. Can I tell you about the meeting though, it's important…'?

'No, keep that until you are here, I'll take a full debrief from you then and we can decide together what the next step to your mission is.'

Frustrated, Alexis knew there was no point pressing the Chief and as he pondered where he was the phone went dead. Replacing the handset, he sat back and took his coffee in short, quick slurps. The door opened again after just a few minutes and Superintendent Sartori entered. She was taller than Alexis with short dark hair, no make-up, he noticed, and her hands were strong with short natural nails. Her face was soft, yet it showed the lines of her tough rise through the ranks of a traditionally male dominated profession, 'I have an officer ready to be assigned to you for the day. He'll take you back to the Vatican City and then after you've finished your meeting, he'll take you to the hotel to collect your bags. We can get you on a plane this evening and have reserved you a seat, I hope that is what you need.' Her voice was strong, and she had an uncompromising manner that Alexis knew didn't allow for poor performance and foolish behaviour.

'Yes, thank you.' He didn't need to say anything else as she turned and left him to the calming warmth of his coffee.

Chapter 24

Morgan dropped the Neerdorf's back at the villa and gauged from the talk in the car that the head of the family was well and truly on the mend. He smiled to himself, happy that Dirk would soon be home, and he could once more serve the man who'd given him the opportunity to start his business a few years earlier. As Erik stepped out of the top of the range people carrier, he turned to Morgan 'thanks again, we appreciate your efficiency.'
'My pleasure Mr Neerdorf, I'm happy to help you and the family whenever I can.' He was always in sales mode and was acutely aware that repeat business of this type was great for business.
'Call me Erik. Can you wait here for a minute though; I want to go into the town and visit the bank'.
'Sure, Erik just let me know when you're ready to go.'
True to his word, Erik came back out of the house after a couple of minutes and got into the back seat. 'Cullis Vaults please Morgan' He closed the door and stabbed some numbers into the keypad of his phone. 'Hello, my name is Erik Neerdorf and I'm on my way to the bank. I'd like to see the CEO please' he listed to the receptionist tell him that wasn't possible at short notice 'well I am on my way and I want to see one of the company directors regarding a deposit my father made a while ago.'
He remained quiet again as he heard how they were all in meetings for the rest of the day, or away on business, or just not available. 'ok I hear what you are saying. Just let your people know that I will have a TV crew and some journalists with me if I can't get to see someone in authority'. He waited as the phone went silent for a few minutes, he then hung up after being told that the CEO had finished his meeting early and could see him for 15 mins.

Arriving outside the heavy-set double doors of the bank, Erik pressed the intercom and introduced himself, waiting a couple of seconds before the lock clicked and buzzed. He pushed the door and entered lobby as the door swung closed behind him. As soon as he sat on one of the seats in the waiting area, a door opened at the back of the circular room and a man appeared 'Mr Neerdorf, welcome to Cullis Vaults, follow me please and I'll take you to see Dominic Hindle, our CEO.' Erik followed, impressed by the understated luxury that filled the building, and as they came to halt outside an office made up of floor to ceiling smoked glass, his escort gently tapped a buzzer on the wall next to the door and spoke into it, 'I have Mr Neerdorf to see you, Dominic'. The door beeped and opened automatically, allowing Erik to enter as his meeting date rose from his seat and walked across the lush, carpeted floor to greet him. 'Welcome Mr Neerdorf, it's good to see you. Come in take a seat, I've arranged some refreshments.'
Erik did as instructed, remaining impressed at the surroundings and the greeting he'd received. It was all very corporate of course and rehearsed time and again to make sure every visitor to this prestigious office was made to feel at ease, and happy to hand over the care of their substantial wealth. 'Thank you, Mr Hindle, that is very kind of you'.
Hindle settled in his seat opposite and took a sip of his coffee. 'So, what can I do for you'. He decided to finish with the pleasantries and get straight to the point.
Erik met Hindle with a steely gaze, also happy to get straight down to business 'I want to know what your bank has done with the $5 million that my father deposited here some weeks ago'. His voice strong and firm, yet calm and friendly.

'Ah, ok. I thought we had resolved this particular matter…'

Not waiting for Hindle to finish his sentence Erik butted in, 'how? How have you resolved matters Mr Hindle? Have you corrected the error and if so, when will the money show in our account?' He tried hard to remain level-headed.

'Mr Neerdorf senior, did not visit this bank at any time over the last six months. He did not deposit any sum of money and we certainly have not made any mistakes with any of our customers' assets.' Hindle stared hard back at Erik, holding his gaze, determined to keep a strong hold of this conversation.

'I have proof that he did'. Erik smiled as he spoke the lie. 'I have CCTV coverage from one of your neighbours that shows my father entering the bank with his case. It also shows him leaving after being inside for half an hour.'

Dominic held his breath for a brief second. He knew that wasn't true because his brother-in-law had assured him that all the CCTV in the area had been checked and any coverage from that day had been deleted. 'Interesting, let me see that footage Mr Neerdorf. If what you have shows what you say it does, then I clearly have a problem with security. However, if as I suspect, what you refer to doesn't exist, I'd like you to finish your coffee and get on with your day'.

Erik knew his attempt to scare the CEO had been amateurish and poorly thought through, annoyed with himself he stood, standing over the desk and looking squarely into Hindle's face he found it impossible not to raise his voice, 'you have stolen our money and I want it back. We aren't going to stop until it is returned, and you and your bank have been exposed…'

Hindle held up his hand, he remained seated and appeared relaxed 'I don't know what fraud you are trying to perpetuate here Mr Neerdorf, but my bank won't be a victim to it. I think your fifteen minutes is up.'

Erik was apoplectic with rage 'you won't get away with this, you're all crooks…'

Hindle pressed a button that was secreted under the lip of his desk, the door opened and two uniformed policemen entered. Hindle stood up and addressed them. 'Take this mad man away and make sure he doesn't get back into my bank'. He turned and wandered to the window, watching the sun dip across the hills in the distance.

The policemen grabbed Erik by the arms and pulled him out of the office and roughly pushed him back through the corridor to a side door. As they opened it one of them looked into Erik's face and spat. 'Don't even think of returning Mr Neerdorf' the words were delivered with venom, 'it won't be very healthy for you or your family if you do.' With that he felt himself falling through the opening onto a soft grass area behind the rear of the bank building. Shaken, he got to his feet and steadied himself, walking back to the pavement he pulled out his phone and called his brother. 'Thomas, we have problem…'.

From his office Dominic watched Erik make his way to the waiting car and he made a call. 'Hi Paul, its Dominic, Erik Neerdorf has just been shown the door, I don't think he'll be returning.'

'Thanks Dominic, that's good news. Appreciate your help as always, speak soon.' Paul put the mobile back in his drawer and recalled with a smile, the day that his cousin was promoted to the top position in a private bank on that small island in Greece.

Chapter 25

The Boeing 787-9 Dreamliner completed its long over-night flight from Amsterdam and made its early evening touch down in Phuket International on time. Roger Barlow collected his luggage and escorted his young companion to the car park where his driver was waiting to take them both on a short drive to the luxury villa Barlow owned near Kamala Beach. Adriana De Haan was just 23 years old but she had worked for Barlow for the last 5 years. She had proved to be one of his best girls and had always been willing to travel to earn the top money and experience the social high life at some of Europe's top venues and high-profile hosts. Barlow had earned plenty of money from her efforts, but he always found her to be very lively and was definitely difficult to manage. He had only sent her to the Vatican because most of the team he ran were occupied that week at other venues and he didn't have anyone else that fit the specific profile that the customer had requested or the experience to fulfil his needs. It was a handsomely paid job; Barlow had no regrets about that part of the assignment, but he definitely wished he'd sent someone else when she broke with protocol and got the press involved. He had a huge problem on his hands now and he still wasn't sure how he was going to resolve it. His contact at the Vatican, Cardinal Hindle had suggested that he pay off Adriana and hide her away for a long period of time. It was a reasonable plan but Barlow knew that he just couldn't trust the girl to stay on the island of Phuket or to keep quiet about how and why she had arrived. The Cardinal wasn't really interested in how the matter was resolved but he wouldn't have relished Barlow's plan B of a quick disposal. There were plenty of places that Barlow knew of where he could hide the girl's body and keep it away from being discovered, maybe even for ever and he wasn't unnerved at the prospect of killing her either; it wouldn't be the first time he'd had to address the problem of an overly confident, indiscreet employee. But there was something about Adriana that set Barlow on edge. He wasn't sure what it was that had his nerves tingling when he considered how he might finish her off and bring this rather unsavoury matter to a close. He had an overwhelming dread however, that it was going to go wrong and this problem she had already created was going to get even worse.

They arrived at the villa after a smooth drive and both visitors entered the palatial home with quite different thoughts. Adriana had taken a while to accept the terms of the deal. After all, she still had friends and some family left back in the Netherlands so spending two years out here in a new world took some thinking over. The cash made it easier of course and her plan was to allow things to settle, see how the land lay in maybe six to twelve months and discreetly make an effort to return home. No-one would know are even care after that length of time and if she had been careful, she would still have enough money left over to keep her going comfortably.

Barlow was keen for the girl to deposit her belongings and join him on a tour of the immediate area. The least amount of time she spent in the villa the better he thought, as her DNA would already have been deposited in the rooms she had walked through. He would need to get the place deep cleaned when he had finished. Barlow had settled on a third plan that he considered to be compatible with both his and his client' needs and had made a few calls to put it into place. All he needed to do was get the girl out into the bustling town that made up this remarkably busy tourist district. 'Adriana' he called through to her bedroom 'I have arranged for us to eat at a local restaurant, it's one of my favourites'. He popped his head around the door. Adriana was led on the bed with her eyes closed 'do we have to? I'm so tired after that flight'. She opened her weary eyes and playfully pouted at him.

Barlow smiled 'come on, you'll feel much better with some good food and a beer inside you'. She slid her feet off the bed and stood up, dramatically feigning her fatigue 'ok, let's go.' The car was still waiting for them and they got back into their seats as it moved off the driveway slowly and into the heavy evening traffic. It stopped outside the Ginger Fusion bar and grill and as they got out, they were greeted by the owner who after warmly greeting Barlow, showed them to a small table in the open-air courtyard with a view of the beach and sea. Adriana was liking what she had seen so far and was starting to think about how well she might settle and get to know some of the locals. Her host and boss was being very warm and friendly too, maybe he had ideas about sampling her services later, not much chance of that though, she had made a firm promise to herself before the journey had begun that she wasn't going to let him near her, not even if he paid. There was something she didn't like about Roger Barlow, she'd always thought him dangerous and difficult to read, a bit slimy too if truth be told but that came with the territory and he was more than twice her age. She accepted that that sort of thinking was almost hypocritical as a lot of her clients were old enough to be her father or even grandfather, but Barlow was the boss, and too close to her business for her to get involved with him.

'You looked like you enjoyed that' Barlow's words stirred her out of her drowsy state, 'delicious' she responded with a wide smile 'the beer is very welcome too. I'm starting to unwind already. What's next on your agenda?' She smiled and Barlow realised why she was one his best income generators. Her face curated a most welcoming and seductive vision, a beautiful picture he thought, and the bright white teeth shone from a smile that was the gateway to her youthful allure. 'I've arranged to meet up with a friend about some business for a few minutes, it won't be long and then we'll see what you feel like doing.' He paid the bill and thanked the waiter, who held the seat as Adriana stood and followed. It was a short walk off the main street and up a side road to what looked like the back entrance to a garage. It was dirty and dusty and as Barlow knocked on the iron covered doorway, it was opened onto a flagged yard by a large local man who looked like an overweight wrestler. He greeted Barlow with the hug of a long-lost brother and beckoned them both inside quickly and as Adriana passed through, the heavy iron door slammed shut with a bang that made her jump. Both men shared a laughed as a third man arrived. He was dressed in a dark suit, white open necked shirt, and smart shiny shoes. 'Roger, how great to see you, my friend.' His voice was clear, authoritarian, and spoken in perfect English, 'and this is the girl?' his question made Adriana shudder and for the first time she realised that she had no idea where she was. 'She is very pretty, much better than you described' he laughed.

Barlow shook the man's hand 'I told you I wouldn't let you down.'

'What is going on here?' Adriana's high-pitched question emphasised her sudden nervousness. Looking at Barlow she trembled slightly, 'just who are these people?'

'The money will be in your account in an hour' The suited man was now looking serious as he addressed Barlow. 'The agreed amount, and a little bit more given that she's incredibly special and will be extremely popular' he laughed again and rubbed his hands together. Adriana looked around, startled, seeking a way out but there was no obvious route. Her heart raced as she tried to come up with a plan of escape. Her instinct told her to run, as fast and as far as she could and off she went, in the opposite direction of the iron door and into a small and narrow corridor with five, closed shabby doors off it. A set of stairs climbed to her right and she considered running up them for a short second but decided against it. She decided to try the furthest door and headed in its direction, hoping that it exited onto some sort of reception and the street beyond. As she moved however, she became aware that the men in the yard had casually followed her and her heart sank. That could only mean one thing, that she was trapped, and they knew that she had no way of escape. She arrived at the cheap wooden door and grabbed the handle, it swung open into a large room with a sealed door across the other side of it, and a large, darkened window that looked out across a bar and at what looked like a lounge, occupied by mostly male drinkers. She stood alarmed, petrified, confused and as she took in the rest of the room, she realised that she had arrived in a sparsely fitted out bedroom with an old bed stuck in the middle and a shower in the corner with a grubby curtain pulled across its cracked and dirty, old tiles. Towels were stacked on a drawer unit next to the bed and a mirror stood full length next to the door. As she turned the suited man appeared, 'like it?' he grinned. 'This one isn't yours I'm afraid but I'll take you up to your room and you can get settled in. You won't be working tonight, so we can take some time to get to know each other'.

'what the fuck are you talking about? ROGER!!' she shouted as loudly as her croaking voice would allow.

'He's gone now Adriana, I'm your new boss, you're mine.' Another leering smile. 'follow me, your new home awaits'.

The 'wrestler' appeared and grabbed her arm and as she struggled, he picked her up and flung her over her shoulder. 'get the fuck off me, what are you doing...'

They went up the staircase she had seen earlier and into a dark room three doors down on the left-hand side of the narrow dimly lit corridor, where Adriana was thrown onto the bed.

The suited man followed 'this will be your room for the next few years. Keep it clean and we'll not fall out. You will live and sleep in here and of course, do your work also. When I think I can trust you, I'll allow you off the premises but for now, get used to it.' He stared at her shivering in fear, sobbing, on the bed 'Oh, and don't think about trying to leave, I have these in my safe keeping' he held up her passport and handbag which contained her phone and purse. Her new 'boss' smiled warmly, his tone was soft and gentle 'I think you'll do well here; my local regulars will adore you. And so will I...' he turned and left the room, closing it behind him. Adriana noticed that he didn't lock it, but then why would he, she had nowhere to go.

Chapter 26

The light blue Fiat Grande Punto looked in good condition as Alexis left the station and opened its passenger door to climb in next to his colleague for the day. As he got in and buckled up the seat belt though, the smell of sweat and old pizza boxes struck him. Alexis glanced into the rear seats and saw with disgust, an array of fast-food boxes, mostly empty, and plastic drinks bottles, newspapers, magazines, and an assortment of other rubbish that made it resemble a refuse skip. 'I know' exclaimed Lou Leoni, the driver, and new aide to Alexis. 'It's a mess and I need to clear it out. It'll get sorted when I get the opportunity, this job takes up all the time I got.'

Alexis doubted it, what happened if this guy actually arrested someone, where would he put them? He chose to ignore it. ' So, Lou, let's get going I need to pick some things up from the Vatican City and have a quick meeting with one of the Cardinals there. We should be half an hour, an hour at the most and then back across the river to my hotel…'

'yeah, yeah, I know the agenda so save it. What are you meeting the Cardinal about?'

Alexis didn't take to the driver at all and wasn't about to enlighten him about the case he was working on. 'nothing too exciting, I'm just following up on a statement he made a while back.'

'exciting enough for you to fly here from Greece though, that can't be cheap.' Lou sneered, hoping for a bit more detail.

'well, you know how it is. One thing links to another and then before you know it there are a million questions to ask' Alexis hoped he was being vague enough to stop the enquiring Italian probing further.

'Yeah, I know that for sure, but if the situation were reversed, there is no way our Commander would sign off a visit to Greece. You lot must have more funding than us, or your Chief's are more relaxed about spending it.' Lou laughed sarcastically as he sped through the busy streets.

'Are you joining me as I interview the Cardinal then?' Alexis initially wanted a witness to the up-coming meeting but having acquainted himself with this officer he now hoped that wouldn't the case as he didn't really want to be seen with this scruffy, unshaven, smelly representative of the local police.

'Nah, my brief is to chauffeur you to where you need to be and then get back to the station later to finish off some paperwork that I've been meaning to get to for a few days.'

Alexis breathed a sigh of relief and then realised that the station had effectively got rid of their problem officer for the day. He wondered how the person next to him had ever got through the selection process and into the force at all, not just that but how on earth had he ever passed a driving test as well. Alexis sat rigid in his seat as the car screamed across town, over the bridge towards their destination at breakneck speed, narrowly missing other cars, scooters, and pedestrians, appearing not to notice or comment about the abuse he was getting, the kerbs he clipped and corners he cut as he drove the Fiat at its limit.

Paul Hindle knocked on the door to De Cathays office and walked in. 'Ah Paul, I understand that the policeman is on his way back to meet us?' Georges' question was really a statement, but Paul answered it non the less. 'Yes Georges, he should be here in a few minutes.'

'Excellent' De Cathay stopped what he was doing 'and what have you got in store for him?'

Paul shuffled uncomfortably 'I haven't been able to coordinate anything with my contacts Georges, there just hasn't been enough time'. Paul held his breath waiting for the backlash in response to his failure.

'ok I understand that Paul, so what is your plan?' Georges eyed his colleague with a menacing look that Paul hadn't witnessed before. It made his blood run cold and he felt a tremor run through his body. 'I thought that we could somehow detain him in the vaults, no-one will know he is there, and I can then address the problem in a day or two'.

De Cathay could sense that Hindle was making it up as he went along and hadn't got a plan at all. 'very disappointing Paulo' shaking his head and moving to his seat. 'Let me tell you what is going to happen shall I?' he stared deeply into the eyes of the shivering man that stood before him. 'SHALL I?' he shouted, catching Paul by surprise, and sending him into a splutter. 'THIS IS WHAT YOU WILL DO.' The shout reverted to a whisper 'take the policeman down into the vaults and kill him'.

Paul's tremble was becoming noticeable 'I can't do that, what will I do with the body?'

'hide it in one of the steel cabinets and if you cannot then manage to get rid of it, I'll arrange for it to be collected and disposed of. I thought you had all of these things covered off Paulo, you're the man with contacts, aren't you?' he sneered and watched the usually calm Hindle try and steady his nerves.

'Georges' he pleaded 'these things take time to organise, I need to ensure confidentiality and there is a cost.'

'just get it done' De Cathays response was dismissive and threatening 'we have too much invested here for some little upstart to ruin it. Get rid of him and we are in the clear but the longer you leave it the greater the risk for us...both'!

'he'll be quickly missed though Georges and then people will be asking questions...'

'no one will be asking any questions; I have made sure that the search for him will not be too intense. I'm not going to discuss this with you for the rest of the day. I suggest you go now; you have a guest waiting.' De Cathay turned in his seat to glance out of the window. 'Still here?' His voice boomed across the room and seemed to vibrate in the very core of Paul's head. He turned and walked out of the room and into the long corridor. He stopped at the large double door and the thought of the last moments of Cardinal De Brazi came rushing back to him, unnerving him even more. Retribution is a cruel and often unkind visitor, especially when delivered by Angels of the Divine.

Paul gathered himself and quickly left for the reception area. Looking out of the window he noticed the police car parked outside with a uniformed driver sat in the driver's seat. He addressed the Swiss Guard on duty 'I'm here to greet officer Demetriou, where is he?' Paul scanned the lobby for his guest and couldn't see him.

'I've put him in the side room with a coffee?' the guard answered quizzically, hoping that he hadn't done anything wrong.

'what is the policeman outside doing, do we know?'

'He is apparently happy to wait out there until Demetriou is finished'.

'ok thanks. Can you go and dismiss him please? Tell him we'll organise a car for Alexis to complete his day.'

The Swiss Guard turned and marched to the waiting Fiat. Lou Leoni didn't need telling twice that his day had suddenly become free, he was more than happy to abandon his Greek colleague and swiftly drive off to get another pizza.

'Alexis, thanks for returning so quickly, I know you are terribly busy, so this is very much appreciated'. Paul strode onto the small waiting room and held out his hand to the seated visitor.

Alexis took the warm hand, noticing that the Cardinal had changed into a full black cassock 'That's not a problem' he responded, rising to greet his host. 'I can't believe how absent minded I was to drop my phone, I just can't exist without it so not returning wasn't an option' he laughed nervously, remember the awkward encounter they had earlier.

'come follow me, I have a surprise for you. I've asked one of the guards to bring your mobile to us and in the meantime, I thought I could give you a quick tour of some of our historical vaults. I know you have an interest, and it would be my way of apologising for the way we spoke to you earlier.'

Alexis was surprised by the friendly offer and wondered where the other Cardinal was. 'will we meet Cardinal De Cathay again?' he enquired tentatively.

'Not this afternoon,' Paul responded 'he has a full diary through the rest of the day and tomorrow. You can relax.' Paul smiled and left the room beckoning Alexis to follow him. With a sense of excitement, he followed trying to keep up with the fast pace set by his host. They veered off the corridor through a steel door into a dark stairwell that led down a few floors. As Alexis looked over the banister, he could see the spirals going surprisingly deep into the depths of this amazing building. 'Where does this lead to?' he asked, raising his voice to the dashing figure in front of him.

Paul paused, sensing the heavy breathing of Alexis behind him 'This is where we store our most precious and ancient articles. Some of the documents here date back to when Christ himself was alive and we have jewels and early Christian items of worship that not many people have actually seen. You're a lucky man Alexis.' Paul gestured him to follow again, just one more flight and we'll be there.

Arriving in what resembled an old stone catacomb measuring about four metres square, Alexis stared in awe at the sights that were in front of him. He had expected the floor to be in a state of ruin given its age, but it had been renovated, sympathetically, and was heated and well lit. There were display cabinets and document holders placed by the walls and he noticed that the stone walls that surrounded were heavily carved with ornate pictures of animals and ancient human figures. Between the cabinets and filing chests there were doors on each wall, and Alexis followed as Paul opened one of them and entered another narrow corridor. The excitement carried him without thinking about where they might end up, his eyes sparkled as it caught the lights and his breath had quickened. Both men walked briskly through what turned out to be a short connecting walkway to another vault that was different to the one they had arrived in just a few moments before. This one was darker and the warmth had disappeared. 'what is this room for?' Alexis enquired, still excited and curious to see what rarity his host was going to show him. 'it's certainly colder' he laughed.

Paul stopped and turned, still smiling 'yes, we need to keep it cooler in here for the sake of the items we store in these cabinets.' He held out his hand gesturing to the block of steel wardrobes that filled one wall in the room and as he circled, he pointed at the floor to ceiling glass display boxes on the opposite wall. 'the lights were faded but increased slightly as the men walked to the edge of the room following the edge of the glass display boxes. Each one of them contained items that Paul explained originated around the time of Christ. Scrolls, items of cloth, gold and silver fishes and some early crucifixes. Hundreds of items that Alexis thought should really be in a museum and available for members of the public. He stood and looked in silence, his heart racing, eyes wide taking in the incredible experience he was being granted. 'How can these amazing things be kept in secret?' he turned to look at Paul.

'They belong to the Church Alexis, some of these things reach back to the very beginning and lay at the very heart of our beliefs. They are the most precious items that exist in the whole world and to put them in front of the public, creates a risk that we just cannot take'.

'Yes, but no-one even knows they are here…'

'No Alexis, we can't allow the existence of these items to become public knowledge. No-one outside of the Vatican hierarchy have been down here, some of the people you have seen today don't even know that this is here.'

Alexis thought on that statement for a second and in an instant, he went from excited to petrified as a strange realisation crept over him. 'So, why show me then cardinal?'

'Because I know you hold a keen interest and I know that you won't be in a position to divulge this secret to anyone else.'

'I'm confused' Alexis started to feel panic 'what do you mean I won't divulge this secret?'

'It's been nice knowing you Alexis, but I fear that your end is nearing'. Paul stood still; his face fixed on the paling police officer.

'I, I think its time for me to collect my phone and get going…please' his stuttering voice broke to a crackle as the sentence petered off.

'Sorry Alexis, that just isn't possible.' Paul pulled the dagger from his cassock and in a single swift movement, pushed it into the chest of the man stood a yard in front of him. The action was quick and left no time for Alexis to move. The dimmed light reflected off the blade and created a weird, surreal sensation as Alexis watched in horror as it struck him and entered his body effortlessly. At first there was no pain, just shock as blood spurted and adrenalin took over. Helpless, he slumped to the floor and the dagger left him. He watched as it rose high into the air above the right shoulder of this man of God and then he screamed as it plunged downwards with huge force, piercing his heart, and turning off his life. Paul Hindle turned, opened one of the steel cabinets and dragged the lifeless body of the policeman across the floor, bundling it into the airtight steel chamber, he closed the door and locked it with the large heavy key that was attached to a silver chain on his belt. He'd clear up the mess later and already had an idea of how and where to dispose of the corpse.

De Cathay picked up his phone and dialled a familiar number 'Officer Demetriou has been dealt with and will not be bothering us anymore'.

'This is good news' the man's voice on the other end sounded appreciative. 'what about the Dutchman, I understand that he is still alive.'

'We have that matter in hand'.

'I'll leave that matter in your capable hands. I'll call off the search for Demetriou in a few days and close the inquiry into Neerdorf's missing cash. The local police can investigate his demise, when that happens but they won't get far, the Chief is lazy and incompetent, and they all just want an easy life.'

'This all sounds like it's coming together nicely, thanks for your help Minister, I'll organise payment to your account in one week, subject to everything being satisfactory.'

'Thank you, Cardinal, I'll call you with a final update when I am able'.

De Cathay cut the call and sat back in his chair, smiling, and feeling relaxed for the first time in a while.

Chapter 27

Paul rose in the morning feeling more tired than at any time in his life. He hadn't really slept at all as the events of the past few days were running around his head adding to his anxiety and stress levels. De Cathay was becoming uncontrollable and irrational and that meant that not only was he capable of making rash decisions, but he was also likely to get Paul embroiled into any enquiries that might ensue and he also had no doubt that De Cathay wouldn't think twice before making Paul the sacrificial lamb. It was all becoming too much, especially after the murder of the policeman and Hindle was feeling ill, unable to eat properly and it was making his general demeanour appear nervous and edgy. He was worried and tried hard to keep himself together as he was on his way for the scheduled meeting with Carla Perez, the new finance chief he had met for the first time a few days earlier. He knocked on her office door and waited, out of courtesy. The heavy wooden door opened, and Carla stood holding onto the ornate handle, smiling warmly, inviting him in.

'Welcome Paul, how nice to see you, can I get you a coffee?' he was taken by her genuine warmth and immediately felt at ease.

After what seemed like a long while chatting pleasantries and drinking the hot double espresso, with a side of ice-cold mineral water, Carla opened a file on her computer screen and turned it to face Paul. He looked at it, trying to make sense of the columns of numbers in front of him. Some of the columns were highlighted in red, others in bold type. 'I give up' he gently laughed 'there is a reason we pay you the big bucks to make sense of this stuff'. He looked up at her and saw she was still smiling 'what does it all mean?' he asked.

'Well in short Paul, this is a snapshot of our financial comings and goings over the past 24 months or so. It's an interesting read in a number of ways but none more so than this extract I've prepared.' She clicked a tab at the foot of the screen. Another spreadsheet opened and Paul noted it was headed 'De Cathay' in bold 'This is a record of what we have spent out of Georges' office over the period'. She paused and looked at Paul. 'It makes for a disturbing read'.

'In what way?' Paul asked, nervously shifting in his seat.

'in an embezzling type of way. She stopped speaking and let the statement sink in.

Paul's mouth was dry, and his brain froze, he couldn't summon up any words, he was simply stunned.

'Yes' Carla continued 'it is rather unbelievable, isn't it?'

Struggling to recover Paul responded, 'that's a profoundly serious allegation Carla, upon what basis are you saying this?'

'Look here' she walked around the desk and stood by him, moving the cursor on the screen she highlighted a single column 'this is a list of all outgoings attributed to his department, and this column' she moved the cursor along 'shows where the payments have gone to. I've followed up each and every one of these and some of them aren't as black and white as they appear.' She clicked a third tab and it opened up into a mass of numbers and colours. 'This is where it gets interesting' she looked at Paul's ashen, tired face. 'This list shows where payments have left us and gone through a web of transfers ending up at a single account. In some instances, there are six or even seven detours before an amount lands.'

'I have limited knowledge of such things' Paul offered.

'It is ok you don't need a deep knowledge of accounting rules, as once you get into this web of different accounts, I only need to show you where it ends up.'

'I'm intrigued' Paul replied truthfully but his stomach was turning, and his head was feeling light.

'There' she pointed at a column heading. 'Pure Life Limited'.

Paul stared, confused. 'What does that mean? I have no knowledge of this business name'.

'No, I doubt that you do, this is a trading name, but you will know the name of the ultimate holding company'.

Paul looked waiting for the bombshell disclosure.

'It's Cat Hay Holdings'.

'never heard of it…' Hindle stopped himself mid-sentence. 'Cat Hay? Cathay? De Cathay?'

'You've got it' she jumped up in delight 'it seems he's been paying himself a fortune for years.'

'I just don't know what to say' Paul sat, stunned at the revelation but then wondered why he was being given this information about someone he had always worked very closely with, some might say even secretly with. 'What are you going to do with this then Carla?'

'Musso is going to see his Holiness with the information and then we will confront Georges. It should be interesting to see his reaction don't you think?'

Paul was still reeling and was surprised at the light-hearted way that Carla was reacting to this most serious of developments. How was Georges going to receive this information, already a man on the edge and how was he, Paul going to be implicated. The dread of the situation bore down on him and he felt his heartbeat faster than he could ever remember, sweat started to bead on his forehead and palms. 'So why tell me Carla? I'm seen as a friend to Georges, is this some sort of test?'

His new colleague walked back around the desk to her seat and sat. She was still calm, and relaxed and friendly. 'Paul, I need to know what you know.'

'I am as surprised as you are about this' he went on the defensive.

'Ah, but I'm not surprised Paul' she laughed. 'When Cardinal Musso first spoke with me about his concerns, I immediately saw some warning signs of financial wrongdoing. It is after all, my job. The scale of it is quite astonishing, that is true, but De Cathay had my predecessor well and truly in a corner and under his control. The man must have been scared out of his wits and that probably contributed to his untimely demise'.

Paul sat listening uncomfortably knowing that what she said was absolutely true. 'I don't know anything about any financial misconduct Ms Perez, I have no knowledge around how Cardinal De Cathay manages his budgets and his financial affairs generally, I just work with him from time to time.'

'Yes, I get that' she replied quickly with a steelier look. 'I have a question though about a large transaction that has taken place in the last few months. I can see that an unusually big withdrawal took place recently only for it to be redeposited again a few days after. What can you tell me about that?'

Paul was struggling now; his breathing was becoming rapid and almost rasping. 'I don't know what you mean, how big of a transaction?' He obviously knew but was playing for thinking time.

'Five million dollars, Paul.' She eyed him for a few seconds, noticing his discomfort. 'Are you ok Paul? You don't look very well.'

He took a few deep breaths 'I know that we corrected a missed payment to a loan we have along with the current months instalment, to bring it up to date, that would have been about that amount.'

She smiled again 'and who were those payments to?'

'We have a draw down facility with a Dutch firm, Neerdorf Securities…'

She cut him off 'ah yes, the infamous draw down. Tell me, why was that arranged in the first place, we have adequate banking facilities with our own finance house?'

Paul thought for a moment, gathering himself. 'I have no idea; I wasn't involved in the placing of it, but I did attend a meeting when the financier called on us to catch up with the debt. That really is as far as my involvement goes.'

Carla paused for a second, observing her work mate and wondered why he was so agitated. She decided to let it go for now. 'Yes, that was Alberto and Georges I understand. There is a complaint being investigated on a Greek island that surrounds the attempted murder of the man who attended your meeting and there is a suggestion that linked to that is the theft of Five Million Dollars. Seems a strange coincidence, that amount being involved, don't you think?'

Paul managed to regain some composure 'I'd heard that too, but I don't know. We had a Greek police officer come to see us about it but all we could tell him was that Neerdorf left with the money and that was the end of it as far as we are concerned.'

'ok Paul, that's enough for now.' She picked up her coffee cup and went to the machine by the window to fill it up. 'Do you want another?'

'No thanks, I'll be on my way if that's all' he went to stand.

'Well, that isn't all Paul, please remain seated' Paul was concerned at the apparent contradiction and was startled by her authoritarian approach, but he sat back down.

'Why did we pay Neerdorf back in cash Paul?'

He was hoping that question would pass him by. 'I wasn't privy to that information although I did query it with Georges'.

'and what did he say?'

'just that it was necessary, and I shouldn't ask too many questions.'

'but that is your job, asking questions is part of protecting the church, Paul.'

'Let me tell you what I can see from that spread sheet. Five Million dollars went out, it came back in a few days later and then that exact amount was dispersed across six different bank accounts before ending up at Pure Life Limited.'

Paul sat in silence, was his time up, had he been caught out. 'I just attended the meeting to support Georges, mine was a corporate hospitality role really, just to meet and greet the guest, shake his hand and show him out. The detail was all Georges, and he did all the speaking'.

Carla returned to her desk and sat back down. 'I've given you a lot of information today Paul. I'm sure I don't need to remind you that all of it is confidential and does not leave this room.'

He nodded 'I don't need reminding; I know my obligations.'

'I'm extremely glad to hear that. Given everything that we've discussed have you informed a view about what has happened with Neerdorf and his money?'

The question caught Hindle off guard a little and he took his time to answer.

'is that too difficult a question Paul?' She again smiled and her relaxed manner unnerved him, as it had done throughout the meeting.

'I have no idea' he lied.

'what, about the difficulty of the question of the Neerdorf situation?'

She was playing with him now and he was even more uncomfortable. 'The Neerdorf question' he responded quietly.

'I have a theory' she picked up her coffee and circled it in her hand whist gazing deeply into the swirling liquid. Paul remained silent. 'I think Georges made the payment in cash with the intention of murdering Neerdorf, stealing back the money and keeping it. But it hasn't gone to plan has it Paul?' She casually glanced over at the sweating, trembling figure across the desk 'Surely not Carla' he manged to croak 'whatever you might think of him, Georges is ultimately a man of God'.

Carla's smile left her face for probably the first time that day 'Paul, this is no man of God, he is evil beyond a doubt and has managed to impregnate these holy walls through collusion with the Devil himself. It is our sworn duty to expose him and deal with him appropriately, and that is what we will do.'

They both sat quietly for a few minutes. To Paul it felt like an hour but eventually, Carla looked up, the warmth returned 'thanks for your time today Paul, if I were you, I'd go a lie down and get some rest, you don't look well.'

At that he stood, and they said their goodbyes as he left the office. Returning to his own workplace he opened it and fell into one of the large leather guest chairs situated inside the door. Closing his eyes, he prayed for his own well being and hoped that Carla and Musso had their sights only on his old friend and not himself. Whatever was to happen, his time with the clergy was coming to an end, the thought of living with the aftereffects of this unholy episode would remain in his head for the rest of his days and he didn't want to be looking over his shoulder all the time, even if he escaped justice, he knew that God would hold him accountable when the time came and he wanted that time to be as far off in the future as possible. Thanks to his friend Georges and some other endeavours, he had been able to amass enough of a pension pot to leave and live a comfortable existence, far away, and that was now his plan.

Carla picked up the phone and dialled Musso. 'He's shaken but I'm not sure if he is involved to any great extent. I think we should keep him under observation and monitor his calls and communications'.

'Thanks Carla, I'm not too bothered about Hindle to be truthful, De Cathay is the rotten egg here and its him who we need to eliminate'.

'figuratively of course.' She laughed.

'I've not decided yet' Musso's response was matter of fact 'the boss hasn't given me a direction yet; he wants to mull it over in respect of how public we need to be with his dismissal. I'm thinking that it might be cleaner to allow him to disappear…one way or another.'

Carla considered the words carefully; she couldn't decide whether Musso's sentiment about eliminating De Cathay was literal. If it was, how did that make him any different to the ungodly man they had spent the last few weeks exposing, she thought. Musso realised by the gap in conversation that she was musing over the words he had spoken 'Carla, don't over-think it, God's will shall be done, and we will protect the Church in the best way we can.'

The phone went down, and she returned to studying her numbers, it was a world she was comfortable with and one she knew inside out.

Chapter 28

Morgan had his assignments clearly worked out in his head for today and they all revolved around the needs of Neerdorf family. He was pleased that they had grown to trust him and appeared to value his service, the income was a huge benefit too and meant that when the family returned home, he could afford to take a few days off and spend some quality time with his partner. Morgan had been promising his fiancé some time away for a few months now and at last they both had something to look forward to. Today was also a pivotal day in the contract with the Dutch family as Dirk, the head of the family had been signed off as fit enough to travel and was returning to the Villa where he would spend a few days before they all decided when to return to Amsterdam. He had dropped Mrs Neerdorf at the hospital earlier that morning so she could help Dirk with packing up his things and thanking the staff. Erik and Thomas stayed back at the house to prepare for the welcome home; nothing too tacky and keep it low key were the instructions from mum. Morgan smiled to himself as he thought about the two men putting up bunting and replenishing the flowers. Pulling into the hospital car park he found it easy to find a space today and chose one close to the entrance. There were a couple of people wandering around the grass area to the side of the main building, mostly chatting on a cigarette break and white coated, official looking types where coming and going out of the big ornamental brick doorway. He was early so sat for a while just people watching and enjoying the warmth of the mid-morning sun and as he did so a small black car entered the car park a little too fast so that when it slowed it threw up gravel and made a skidding sound that made everyone around turn to look. It was clearly a hire car and the fact it was small, obviously at the cheaper end of the rental scale, made the occupant look ridiculously large. Morgan watched as the giant of a man extracted himself from the drivers' seat and out of the door, he was carrying a small leather medical bag and grabbed a white coat off the passenger seat. Struggling to put the coat on he quickly walked towards the hospital entrance and disappeared from sight. Allowing Lou Reed to finish telling the world about his perfect day, Morgan got out of the car and strode towards the private rooms to collect his passengers. Making his way into the corridor he stopped at the reception desk to enter his details in the visitor book, noticing that not many people followed the same protocol. He was only the second one today and a thought about the generally lax security flitted through his head as he nodded and smiled to the busy receptionist. As he approached the private room that the Neerdorf's had use of for some time now, he wondered how much the facility had cost the family and whether they had any form of insurance to pay some of those costs. It would be way beyond his means that's for sure. Casting that from his mind he concentrated on presenting a joyful image to the husband and wife who must be overjoyed at finally reaching the day when Dirk was deemed fit and well enough not only to look after himself but to leave the hospital and return home. Morgan knew that they had decided to get back to Amsterdam at the earliest opportunity and so his engagement was also coming to an end. He'd miss them but felt that he'd delivered a first-class service that would lead to more work in the future, and the current assignment was well paid so he would be able to take that long awaiting break as soon as the family had returned to the Netherlands. As he neared the door, he saw the silhouette of what appeared to be a large built doctor on the other side. Morgan couldn't recall seeing anyone around the hospital that resembled such an outline, maybe it's a specialist brought in to oversee the discharge of the patient he thought. Hovering outside for a few seconds, pondering whether to knock on the door or wait for the doctor to finish his duties the unmistakable sound of a silenced gun firing off two quick rounds shook Morgan to the core. The 'thud thud' noise followed instantly by smashing glass was astonishingly, horribly coming from the Neerdorf's room. The two seconds of silence seemed to carry on for ever as time just stood still and Morgan struggled to understand what was happening. The panicked shouts from Neerdorf shook him out of his temporary paralysis and he lunged fearlessly at the door, opening it and barging in to see the man in the white coat stood steady and taking aim at Dirk Neerdorf. Morgan flung himself at the huge frame of the gunman just as he fired off another shot, but losing his balance the bullet caught the window, smashing the pane and sending shards outwards onto the pathway beyond. Even with his physique, Morgan was tiny against the gunman who pushed him off with little effort but in doing so lost grip of the gun and they both watched it silently as it slid deep under the bed. The alarms in the hospital were now howling loudly and there was no doubt that the emergency services had been notified and would be here in minutes. The gunman made the decision to run and off he went pushing the medical and security staff out of his way as he went as quickly as his thick legs would carry him, to the parked, unsuitable hire car he had arrived in, 20 minutes earlier. Morgan was in a daze as a duty doctor entered the room, followed by two nurses, the receptionist and then Dawson McKeown the Chief Medical Officer. One of the nurses led Morgan to the large leather chair in the corner and helped him sit down and clear his head. As he sat and his vision returned, he saw the carnage that he had thrown himself into just moments before, and amongst it all, laid out on the floor with a pool of blood streaming from a huge wound in the back of her head was Katherine Neerdorf, unmistakably dead. The doctor took a sheet and covered her up instinctively and out of respect. Morgan moved his head to survey the rest of the room and his eyes settled on Dirk, curled up tightly in the corner, shielding behind the bed frame sobbing uncontrollably. Dawson McKeown was knelt beside him, trying to console this man who had been through so much over the past few months, a man who had just witnessed the cold bloodied murder of his wife. No one in that room had any room for thoughts, the trauma was just too much, they were all numb and completely in shock. Dirk Neerdorf in his stunned paralysis was helped to move by McKeown and was sedated in an adjoining room, and then the police, already in their all-white protective suits, boots and masks started to document and photograph the murder scene and its dead occupant.

Morgan sat and stared blankly at all this unfolding before him, tears welling up in his eyes as he started to shudder, his whole body shaking, gripping the arms of the chair so his knuckles showed white. The whirring of the sirens introduced the arrival of even more police and before long the whole hospital was a manic explosion of frantic activity yet, Morgan felt nothing as he watched a nurse talking to him, but he couldn't understand the words. She held his arm and he followed as though on rails, he had no control over his actions, his head was just empty. He was guided towards a bed where he sat. The nurse swung his legs up onto the mattress and gently helped him lay back and then he observed her prepare a needle which she injected smoothly into his arm and then…sleep.

Chapter 29

The phone rang on De Cathays desk almost at the same time as the mobile in his top drawer. Opening his drawer and glancing at the display he decided to answer the landline. It was Cardinal Musso who spoke as soon as the call connected and without any pleasantries. 'Georges you're in then?' the obvious sarcasm put him immediately on edge, it wasn't really a question and De Cathay didn't offer a response. 'Stay in your office please, I am on my way to see you and need to discuss some very important matters that have arisen. I'll be ten minutes' The phone went dead without Georges saying a word. He returned the receiver and sat for a second feeling uneasy.

Opening his drawer, he picked up the mobile phone which disclosed the missed call to be from the Police Commissioner's office in Rome. He pressed the call button and switched to speaker mode, placing the phone on the desk in front of him he picked up a pen and readied himself to take notes. 'Georges we have a situation developing' the Commissioner sounded breathless as though he had been running but Georges knew that hadn't happened for a long time.
'What is the problem my friend?' De Cathay sounded calm but his heart was racing 'whatever has happened can be resolved, so calm down a bit and talk to me' he was hoping the smile and warmth on his face had transferred to his voice.
'our Greek colleagues have stopped a man fleeing from a shooting at the Hospital in Kos, he is admitting to the murder of Mrs Neerdorf and the attempted murder of Mr Neerdorf.'
De Cathay gasped and closed his eyes tightly,' Neerdorf still isn't dead' he thought to himself. 'And what has that got to do with either of us?'
The Commissioner held his breath for a few seconds, 'Well, he has named you as being the one who ordered and paid for it to happen.'
Georges tensed up 'so I repeat, what has this got to do with either of us?' He decided to ride it out 'some crazy murderer is trying to deflect responsibility of his psychotic actions by throwing the name of a high profile dignitary into the mix. There is nothing in it I'm sure' he managed a short chuckle to support the lie.
'He's showed them a bank statement showing a payment that emanates from what my colleagues call a known account.'
'That can be forged quite easily, listen to me…'
The Commissioner butted in before Georges could finish 'they also have a recorded conversation of you telling the assassin how to make the call after the shooting and when he could expect the balance of his money. It's your voice Georges, and the phone traces back to your department'
De Cathay held his thoughts for a moment, he remembered making the call, but it was on an encrypted phone. The realisation that he had been caught came very quickly and he slumped back in his chair. The lines on his ashen white face becoming deeply etched and his mouth suddenly went bone dry. 'what will happen?'
'I have no choice my friend, you will be arrested to answer the charges, but I'll do what I can to make it easy for you. I'd guess you have two hours before they arrive'
'OK I'll be ready for them, thanks for the alert'

'That is ok Georges, you have looked after me over the years, so I owe it you. Just one more thing before they arrive, make sure you transfer the balance of my money to my account please.'

De Cathay switched the mobile off and placed it in a secret safe above the ceiling tiles at the rear of his office. Even after he was long gone, no-one would find it there alongside the incriminating documents and photo's he had accumulated and stored over the years.

The office door opened just as De Cathay sat back down at his desk and Musso stormed in.

'come in Eduardo, how nice to see you' Georges spoke calmly in spite of the phone call he had just had and sending the sarcasm straight back at his adversary 'sit down, make yourself comfortable'

'I'll stand' Musso retorted as he took a position in the centre of the room facing his seated colleague 'so, Georges, it's been an eventful few days hasn't it?' he looked hard and cold, directly into the watery red eyes across the desk.

'eventful?' Georges questioned 'for whom?'

'well, for all of us and I find myself in a rather fortunate position' his face broke with an almost evil smirk and he continued without letting De Cathay intervene further 'the net is closing Cardinal De Cathay,' he spat the words with venom 'I, we, have enough evidence of your embezzlements. Theft from the Holy house, from God himself. We can see everything you've taken and where you've sent it over the years you've been in office, we have evidence of the terror you have caused to some of your colleagues and the inexcusable mis-use of power you exerted over them to get your own wicked way. We can also connect you to the terrible events that have befallen the poor Neerdorf family over the last few months. You're finished…' Musso took breath and watched De Cathays reaction to his tirade. But De Cathay didn't respond, he just sat, listening, head bowed slightly, arms relaxed by his side. After a short silence he looked up smiling 'Cardinal Musso' Georges spoke softly and into the room rather than directly at the man taking up the centre of his office. 'You are everything that is wrong with the modern-day church, you're a dinosaur living in the past. You and your type are the reason our beloved church is dying a death, it'll all be gone in 20 years' time and people around the globe will look back and see I am right. You will answer to God and He will not be pleased with the way you and your cohorts have let the faith go to ruin. We used to be all powerful and our work stretched across the whole world into every dark corner. Our word saved civilisations and created Saints, it was an honour and a privilege to be around the head of it, seeing the good we were doing and receiving the appreciation of our vast number of followers. But it's gone, a rapid decaying decline caused by the inability of people like you to change and modernise and recognise the needs of a modern population' he stopped and with bubbling moisture in his eyes, looked Musso in the face 'all I have done, in all my time serving our Lord, is try to protect Him and help spread the glorious word of hope and salvation. Do what you need to do but I will not be blamed for the misguided leadership that has brought us to this pathetic point in our splendid history' Musso stood in astonishment and disgust at what he was hearing 'You have no remorse over what you have done and continue to do? Lining your own pocket at the expense of other people and to the detriment of our beloved church. You, De Cathay, are in cahoots with the devil himself and the world will be significantly better off when you are rotting in jail. I am authorised to tell you to clear your desk and expect the Guard in half an hour to escort you to a cell, where you will await a hearing and a move to prosecute you in the courts. It's a good day for the Church De Cathay, because you are no more'. At that Musso moved to the door and slipped out into the corridor, closing the ancient solid oak exit behind him, he stopped and steadied himself against the cold stone wall. Breathing deeply he smiled broadly, clenching his fists in victory, sensing his elevation further up the ranks of this Holy order that he had sacrificed his whole life to and he was now looking forward to reaping the rewards of his personal and emotional sacrifices and to the power and the glory that were surely coming his way.

Chapter 30

Hindle couldn't believe what he was hearing. The gunman had gained access the private room at the hospital, unloaded his automatic pistol and still failed to silence Dirk Neerdorf. What is protecting this man he thought, accepting the irony almost immediately, how many lives does he possess? Paul sat back in his deep leather chair after the call and screwed his eyes tight. How will De Cathay receive this news he wondered, what violent reaction would Paul witness next from his deeply and worryingly erratic colleague. The phone rang on his desk and the display showed G D-C. Paul hesitated slightly, his heart pumping and heat rising in his neck and face, then picked it up 'hello Georges, how are you?'
'I'm ok thanks Paul, I wondered if you'd mind coming over to my office, I need to speak with you'
Paul heard the stress in De Cathays voice and held his breath. He desperately didn't want to be involved in whatever Georges was cooking up next. The silence must have gone on for longer that Paul imagined. 'Paul, are you there? I need to see you my friend, as quickly as you can please'
'Yes, sorry Georges, I'll be right with you' he put the phone down feeling sick and desperately disappointed that he hadn't stuck to his guns. He left immediately thinking about what was about to greet him but also something at the back of his mind nagged at him that Georges wasn't in fact ok and that the tone of his voice had an edge he hadn't witnessed before. One thing was certain, all of this was getting too much for Paul and he couldn't wait to set the ball in motion for his leaving office. He would address that later today or tomorrow but for now he braced himself as he knocked on the familiar wooden door. The voice on the other side beckoned him in and as he gently eased the heavy door open and stepped in, the large office looked, as always, every bit the opulent expansive domain of one of the most superior officers of this two thousand year old business. State of the art technology clashed with ancient artefacts and iconography and residing in it, sat at a two hundred-year-old, solid oak ornate desk was the giant frame of a weary, pale, beaten looking man. De Cathay sat in his purple cassock with heavy a gold crucifix around his neck, hands clasped and placed on the desk in front of him. Paul reeled in shock at the sight before him 'Georges, you look…'
'Yes, I do Paul, awful is the word I think you are looking for, maybe shattered or even defeated'
Paul stepped quickly over to the desk 'let me help you Georges, what do you need?' his offer was one of comfort, solace, or to provide medical assistance even but De Cathay looked on with heavy eyes 'it's all over Paul, I am being ousted and the police are on their way to arrest me…'
Paul shook with horror and immediately thought about the policeman's body he had earlier arranged to be moved. What if the authorities knew about that, what if he was on the list to be arrested too?
Georges saw the look of panic and instinctively knew what was going through his compatriots mind 'you need not be worried my friend; no harm will come to you. I have taken all responsibility for the events that have taken place and you are not implicated.'
Paul relaxed slightly but the concern for his colleague was growing 'what are you being arrested for?'
Georges shrugged 'it matters not but I didn't ask you to come here to discuss this, I need you to do one last for me'

Paul looked on, shaking slightly and pale yet the sweat was building on his forehead and dampening his palms 'what can I do?' he offered quietly

'I have a safe place in this room Paul, it contains paperwork that I have accumulated over the years. Agreements, contracts, contacts. References, phone numbers, ID's and serial numbers. I want you to have it Paul, take it all and keep it away from here. In time you will find value in it and it will help keep you into your later years.'

Paul was stunned into silence; he had heard the rumours of De Cathays secrets store but no-one believed it actually existed. Georges pointed to the corner of his room, and up at the tiled ceiling 'I've left it open. Empty the contents into the holdall behind the curtain and get out of the building before the police arrive. If they find you with it, you will be arrested too so be quick.'

At that Paul, dragged a chair into the room, stood on it and lifted the tile. He could see it was loose and as he pushed it up and across onto the other tiles, he saw a wooden casket, anchored to the beams and displaying a digital lock that was flashing green. The door was opened as Georges had said so Paul pulled the door open and saw a mass of paper and files. 'Quickly' Georges rasped behind him. Without stopping to look at the contents he filled the holdall and over the next 10 minutes emptied the secret safe of everything that it held including rolls of cash. Some of the files he noticed were very old, colour faded and delicate whilst others were quite recent, clean and newly marked with dark pen. He quickly closed the casket door so the light went out and carefully replaced the tile so it fit snuggly into the frame before steadily getting off the chair, turning to Georges who looked like he had aged even more in the last fifteen minutes, 'what now?'

De Cathay struggled to his feet and held his arms out wide 'we say our goodbyes my friend. Our time here has been good, we have achieved many things but alas, not everyone agrees with our approach. Its time for us to do what we need to do Paul so you get going and take care' They embraced for a second before Georges let go 'grab the bag a get going, hurry and once you are outside stop for no-one until you get home and can hide the bag until you have some time and you're ready to explore the contents.'

'what about you Georges…'

'Go, you haven't got time' De Cathay fell back into his chair and Paul grabbed the holdall and bolted for the door. He got to his car and put the bag into the boot, quickly jumped into the drivers' seat and pulled out of the main entrance, following directions South onto the Via Della Fornaci and out of the city. He missed the police entourage by a matter of minutes but heard the sirens as they raced over the bridge and towards the Holy City. Less than an hour later, Paul was sat alone in the garden of his family home with a large glass of Chianti. The holdall was safely stored in one of the outhouses that sat within the walls of the estate where Paul had decided to leave it until the dust had settled on the carnage that was about to ensue following De Cathays arrest. In the meantime, he'd return to the office tomorrow and see what lay in store for him.

Four marked police cars entered through the side entrance of the Vatican City and slid to a halt on the gravel floor covering. The Swiss Guard had been alerted that the police were about to appear but even then, everyone in the vicinity were startled at the noise and aggression displayed by the arrival. As the police cars came to an abrupt halt two or three officers alighted from each car and then waited as an unmarked dark red Alfa Romeo rolled into the car park and stopped in a designated bay. The Commissioner got out and walked to the main entrance to be greeted by a guard, whilst the other officers followed with great enthusiasm. 'Take me to Cardinal De Cathay's office please' the commissioner spoke with authority and urgency. Without a word the guard turned and marched the men down the unusually quiet corridors, passed the works of art that adorned the ancient and ornate walls and arrived at the large wooden door with the brass plate that announced the occupant. Before the guard had chance to knock, the commissioner pushed in front of him, holding his hand high 'I will do that thank you' looking hard at the Swiss Guard, bedecked in his strange uniform and dismissed him with a sweep of his hand. Turning to address the gathered officers 'I will enter with you and you' pointing at the two officers who were closest 'the rest of you wait and make sure that no-one enters or leaves any of these offices in this corridor'. Not sure why, they just nodded and relaxed, some wandered back to cover the other doors whist the rest remained. The commissioner grabbed the door handle, took a deep breath and swung it open, rushing into the large office with the two men. 'This is the police Cardinal De Cathay and you are…' the sight that greeted them stopped all three of them in their tracks, and all three stood stock still in shock as they saw Georges De Cathay hanging lifeless by his neck from a rope that was secured to the ancient joists, a chair was sprawled across the floor, De Cathays arms were limp and dangling by his side and wrapped around his left hand was a set of wooden rosary beads. Clearly dead, the mans head was slumped forward and his eyes were bulging wide, appearing to be looking at the golden crucifix sat against his huge chest and oddly, a stream of blood trickled down the cassock and was forming a pool on the floor. The three officers stood still for a few seconds before one of them screamed for their colleagues to come in and help support the frame whilst he grabbed the chair and jumped on it to get at the noose. As the men lifted De Cathays corpse by its legs, the rope slackened and the officer tried to loosen the bloodied rope, he struggled and as he pulled harder at it he saw that three nails were protruding through the rope and into the neck of the dead man. It was clear that he had no intention of being saved.

Chapter 31

Three weeks later Carla Perez met Eduardo Musso at a small café about a mile from Amsterdam's Schiphol airport. She entered and saw Musso already sat at a table in the corner with a coffee. He stood and they hugged warmly before the waiter arrived and took their order for food and more coffee. 'So, Carla, how did your meeting with Mr Neerdorf go, was he pleased to see you?' Musso smirked
'at first he was very apprehensive, unsurprisingly and his sons were quite hostile but after a while they agreed to our terms and signed the document.' She took a folder out of her case and handed it over the table.
'That is excellent work Carla, well done. When will the money be back in their account?'
They will have the five million dollars before the end of today and the remaining draw down will be closed next month when we pay the last instalment.'
'and the NDA?'
'that is included in the folder too. We can safely say that the whole unfortunate episode is now finished'.
Musso smiled as the waiter delivered two plates of rookworst and toast with lattes. He placed the folder into his own case and congratulated Carla again on the work she had done since joining the team. As they finished, he checked his watch 'you have a plane to catch' he motioned at his wrist 'have a good flight back to Rome and I'll see you in a few days'.
'oh, I though we were travelling together?'
'No there was as change of plan, I have another meeting here in half an hour and then I have a flight to London to attend to some of our business over there before I get back before the weekend.'
Carla knew not to ask any more questions. The two of them stood and embraced again, Carla thought that Eduardo held on just a little too long and she wasn't overly enthused at the kiss he placed on her mouth before letting go. She stepped out of the café and crossed the road, ducking into a little side street she stopped and waited a few minutes watching the door of the café to see Paul Hindle walk in, dressed in casual jeans and a short sleeved shirt. As he entered, Musso stood and stuck out his hand 'Paul, how good of you to join me, can I get you a drink, some food?'
'I've eaten thanks Eduardo and I'm really ok for a drink, I need to catch a train in an hour...' he left the sentence open as he took a seat.
Musso sat too and studied the man opposite who he thought looked gaunt and tired 'so you've retired then Paul, Paulo' he grinned as the variation of his name hit home. It was what De Cathay used to call him when he needed a special favour 'Yes Eduardo, thank you for smoothing the way for me, it was very good of you'
'that's fine it was my pleasure, you have served us well and I think you have earned a rest. So, what are your plans?'
Paul sensed a tension in the air, what was Musso up to he wondered. 'Nothing much' he lied 'I will take some time at home to relax and then I might do a little sight-seeing around Europe' he smiled 'so what's this about Eduardo, what do you want from me?'
'As cynical as ever I see' Musso chuckled and waited for a few seconds 'I need to know that I can rely on you Paul, if I ever need your help'
'Help? What sort of help? I've retired Eduardo'

'Retired?' Musso emphasised the word 'it's a funny state that isn't it. In my experience, people with your background and contacts rarely actually really retire. They can't you see, too much history, too much baggage. I think that you'll be forever looking over your shoulder Paul, that's my guess or at least, forever wondering how secure the guarantees were that Georges gave you before he sadly passed away.'

Paul glared across the table 'you're threatening me?' he quizzed

'I'm a man of God, I don't threaten people Paul.'

'So, what is it then, get to the point'

'You have some strong contacts and I just need to know that you aren't taking them all with you, to wherever you are going. I see them as useful and really they are the property of the Church so, I just need to be sure that whenever I need to use one of our contacts' he paused for a second 'that you will be on hand to broker whatever arrangement I need'.

Paul sat amazed at what he was hearing.

'Let me be absolutely clear Paul, you haven't left the Church for good, you are…let's say in a semi-retired state. I'll continue to pay you a consulting fee, you will remain in regular contact and accessible and we will all be very happy. Don't you think, Paul?'

Hindle stood 'you know where I am, I'll wait to hear from you'. He turned and walked out onto the busy street. Having rid himself of a maniac he wondered how much of a tyrant his new boss would be.

Chapter 32

After landing at London Heathrow Airport later that day, Musso got a connecting plane to Rio de Janeiro. He took his seat next to what appeared to be a married German couple who were travelling back to Brazil after a short break in England, seeing the sights. Shortly after take-off and grabbing a sandwich and a drink the three struck up a casual conversation about their movements of that last few days. The Germans had loved London and all of its sights, but the weather was so unpredictable. They were very much looking forward to getting back to Rio where they had made their home. Eduardo talked about Amsterdam and its rich history, the famous canals and architecture, and hinted at some of the seedier elements that can be found in and around the city centre. He then spoke about his beloved Rome and the Holy City that sat within it 'I think you two would love it' he suggested.

'yes, we have been before, but it was a while ago. We'd love the opportunity to revisit.'

'good, I can put you up in Rome's city centre for a few days and then for a short break, I can organise a trip to the beautiful Greek island of Kos.'

The couple smiled in acknowledgment 'such a kind offer, we'd be delighted to accept, thank you so much. Can you recommend any excursions for us?'

Musso leaned across the seats and handed Anita a hand-written note 'this will keep you entertained I dare say'

'The Germans looked down and grinned 'what about expenses?'

'I can keep the usual arrangement and the money can be in your bank account before you leave Kos'

'Excellent, in that case we will be very happy visit next month'

Anita looked down at the note again. It read 1) Commissioner of Police in Rome 2) CEO of Cullis Vaults (KOS).

Having committed the note to memory, she tore the paper up and placed the bits in the remains of her coffee which was then collected and disposed of by the cabin crew.

Happy that their business was concluded, Eduardo Musso sat back, closed his eyes and drifted off into a deep sleep so he was prepared for the return journey, direct to Rome the following day.

The German couple kissed and maintained their appearance of being happily married, delighted that they had managed to keep their jobs.

As they dozed, the inter flight entertainment system informed everyone that 99 red balloons were floating out across the horizon.

The End.

Printed in Great Britain
by Amazon